To Geo

We're

Jim August 2012

Six Political Illusions

Six Political Illusions

*A Primer on Government for
Idealists Fed Up with History Repeating Itself*

James L. Payne

Lytton Publishing Company
Founded 1975
Sandpoint ❖ Idaho

Cover Art: Thomas Cole, *The Voyage of Life: Youth* (1842), Alisa
Mellon Bruce Fund, image courtesy National Gallery of Art,
detail.
Cover Design: Heather McElwain

Lytton Publishing Company
Box 1212
Sandpoint, Idaho 83864
www.LyttonPublishing.com

Contents

Introduction

The Paradox of Big Government

America, the frontier of noble ideals and new departures, has been engaged in a long experiment with big government. For the first century of the country's existence, the federal establishment was little more than a desk and a chair in the wilderness: a small army and navy, a tiny patent office, and the Library of Congress. Then, around the turn of the twentieth century, reformers came forward with the idea of using government to fix society's problems, and the federal government began to grow until it has become very, very large.

These early activists were enthusiastic about using government as the national problem solver. In 1889, Edward Bellamy—whom we shall meet again later in these pages—published the utopian novella *Looking Backward,* which postulated a country run from top to bottom by the federal government. This government's supervision was assumed to be so wise and compassionate that "No man any more has any care for the morrow, either for himself or his children, for the nation guarantees the nurture, education, and comfortable maintenance of every citizen from the cradle to the grave."

His book sparked the formation of scores of "Bellamy clubs" and led a flood of other authors to pen their versions of big-government utopias. There was, so to speak, not a cloud in the sky of the vision of salvation through government. The many activists differed among themselves about details, but they all were fired up with the vision of a nation wisely and fairly managed by government.

Their enthusiasm found its way into policy. The Teddy Roosevelt and Woodrow Wilson administrations refocused the federal government as the nation's comprehensive problem solver, and since then just about every administration has contributed to the expansion of government's reach.

What do Americans think about this experiment with big government? They appear to hold two opposite opinions at the same time. On the one hand, the vision of salvation by government has indeed grown clouded, and the enthusiasm has waned. Americans now mistrust and disparage big government. One sign of the lack of confidence has been the decline of ideological left-wing political parties. Gone are the Bellamyites, the Progressives, the socialists, and the Communists. Today, if anyone were to announce that government can achieve utopia, he or she would be considered childishly naive. Opinion polls mark the same loss of conviction. Generations ago Americans had great confidence in the federal government and a high opinion of its officials' honesty and capacity. In 1958, three-quarters of Americans said that they trusted the government in Washington to do the right thing just about always or most of the time. Today, the proportion having this level of trust has declined to one-quarter of the population.

Yet the great paradox of modern politics is that this skepticism about government has not led people to rely less on it. Former Federal Reserve chairman Paul A. Volker notes the strange contradiction: "Nothing is more certain in American political life," he writes, "than complaints about the performance of the federal government. At the same time, there are insistent demands for government to do more—to provide more security, personal, national, and financial; to improve health care; to protect the environment; to build transport systems."

This remarkable inconsistency about government prevails among all classes of people, from untutored, apathetic citizens to highly educated participants. "Here in Washington," says one speaker, "we've all seen how quickly good intentions can turn into broken promises and wasteful spending." This speaker is not a crusty conservative, pleading for a return to the limited government of yesteryear, but President Barack Obama. In the very same speech in which he made this comment deploring government's wasteful spending and broken promises, however, he urged a great expansion of the federal government, a $787 billion "stimulus" bill that funneled increased spending to government agencies and programs. He urged this new spending, as he took pains to say in his prepared speech, "not because I believe in bigger government—I don't." Here is the paradox of big government voiced by the nation's first citizen: I don't believe in big government, but I want more of it.

New York lawyer and political activist Phillip Howard is deeply disappointed with how government works. In 1994, he wrote *The Death of Common Sense: How Law Is Suffocating America*, a book that harshly criticizes the vast web of modern government regulations. All this regulation does more than cause enormous waste, he says; it "crushes our goals and deadens our spirits."

He cites dozens of cases of government regulation that have produced harmful results. For example, Mother Teresa's Missionaries of Charity wanted to remodel a burned-out building in New York City for a homeless shelter. They didn't want and would refuse to use an elevator, but regulations insisted they spend the extra $100,000 to put one in. The impasse led the nuns to give up on the project—an absurd outcome in Howard's view. "There are probably 1 million buildings in New York without elevators. Homeless people would love to live in almost any one of these."

What's the way to prevent this kind of regulatory mischief? The obvious answer is to get government out of the position of deciding things such as who must have an elevator—or, put more broadly, to make big government smaller. This elementary solution is beyond this expert on "common sense." Howard praises the "effective action" of Franklin Roosevelt's regulatory-rich New Deal and firmly believes that government should be involved in *everything*—education, health, business, environment, product safety, housing, and more.

The passage of time has done nothing to alert Mr. Howard to the painful contradiction between his anger at big government and his commitment to it. In April 2009, fifteen years after *The Death of Common Sense* appeared, Howard wrote an op-ed in the *New York Times* lambasting the medical malpractice liability system, which, he said, "terrorizes doctors," "corrodes relationships with patients," and contributes to waste in the health care system "upwards of $1 trillion per year."

But stop a moment. The medical liability system is a government program. Government sets the rules and limits for it, government courts apply it, and government police implement the courts' awards. Therefore, government itself might scale back its liability system in a dozen ways: by limiting awards, by limiting lawyers' fees, by limiting the time period for complaints, and so on.

None of these solutions occurs to Howard, who appears to be unable to contemplate any kind of government downsizing. Instead, he recommends *more government!* He proposes that Congress create a system of "health courts" to deal with medical malpractice. His faith that this new government system would be fair, prompt, and cost effective is astonishing. Despite having spent decades documenting how even well-intentioned government programs go awry, Howard has faith that *this* new program will work just fine. He doesn't like how government works, but he wants more of it.

This inconsistent attitude toward big government is a worldwide pattern. The public in all countries is generally critical of national leaders and skeptical about government's capacity to operate successfully. Yet this same public is eager for government to take a bigger role in addressing every problem that attracts its notice, from transportation to scientific research, housing, and labor relations.

In 1853, the British commentator Herbert Spencer noticed the inconsistency in England of his day: "Take up a daily paper and you will probably find a leader [op-ed] exposing the corruption, negligence, or mismanagement of some State-department. Cast your eye down the next column, and it is not unlikely you will read proposals for an extension of State-supervision. . . . Ever since society existed Disappointment has been preaching, 'Put not your trust in legislation'; and yet the trust in legislation seems scarcely diminished."

The Role of Illusions

To explain the paradoxical view of big government, we need to understand what lies behind the two contradictory perspectives, distrust on the one hand and longing on the other. It's rather easy to see where the distrust comes from. It is due to failure—or as Spencer put it, "Disappointment." Government programs go awry again and again and often in quite catastrophic ways. In recent times, the public has witnessed the savings-and-loan scandal and bailout, security lapses that led to the terrorist acts of September 11, 2001, flawed intelligence that led to the Iraq invasion, inept responses to Hurricane Katrina, the space shuttle *Columbia* disaster, negligent medical care of veterans, and the subprime mortgage meltdown and the bankruptcy of the government lending agencies Fannie Mae and Freddie Mac. Beyond the high-profile breakdowns are innumerable failing programs that come to light as reporters and scholars—such as Philip Howard—dig behind the scenes in defense, welfare, agriculture, homeland security, environment, energy, job training, and other areas.

When we look more broadly across the world and down through history, government malfunctions are even more noticeable. Governments have plunged countries into appalling wars, carried out shocking genocides, ruined economies, and killed writers and artists. Bad governments rank above plagues and earthquakes as enemies of the human race.

So there's plenty of reason to be skeptical about government. The question is, Why doesn't this skepticism lead people to turn away from big government? Some commentators attempt to explain the growth of government by pointing to a school system that indoctrinates each generation of students into wanting more government. Another factor might be the array of special-interest groups and government officials who enjoy government benefits and who lobby to ensure an ever-increasing flow of tax dollars into their pockets.

There is an element of truth to these explanations. Most teachers tend to be progovernment and to pass their views on to their students. Self-interested officials and special interests certainly do play a role in defending and increasing appropriations. However, I do not believe that such factors are the main explanation. Schoolteachers, politicians, and pressure groups would not have succeeded in fostering big government if people in general were not already receptive to it.

I believe that big government's appeal despite its numerous failures lies in a set of illusions about what government is and what it is capable of accomplishing. I choose the term *illusion* advisedly. The errors I point to are not mere mistakes—errors of fact or simple misinformation. They are impressions that the naive mind has when first presented with the phenomenon of government. They are like the impression of a flat earth gained from looking across a prairie. The land does indeed look flat, and if someone tells you it's not, your mind retains the impression of flatness. But first impressions are important, and these impressions retain a hold even in the mature mind.

Government is a gigantic, complicated structure that has no counterpart in our daily lives and personal experiences. As soon as we hear about it, we start forming opinions, opinions based on first impressions and naive assumptions. These opinions are illusions, ideas that are fundamentally false and misleading, but that nevertheless become embedded in our personal worldview.

When the untutored mind first contemplates government, fragmentary perceptions make it seem that government really is a wealthy, powerful, and effective problem-solving institution. A child just becoming aware of government and public policy will normally say that government should fix things and take care of us. His mind produces this opinion in just the way that it produces the opinion that the world is flat.

As he matures, he begins to overcome the illusions. He gains more knowledge about government, and he also brings to bear his own innate "illusion-busting" cognitive abilities. This process of maturation produces, in the typical case, political views that are a mixture of the underlying illusions and more sophisticated understandings. The illusions are no longer accepted in simple, unvarnished form, but they still influence thinking about what government should do and what it can accomplish.

In the National Gallery in Washington, D.C. hangs a spectacular painting by the American landscape painter Thomas Cole, a panel that depicts in allegory the theory I'm presenting here. Titled *The Voyage of Life: Youth,* it shows a young man cruising in a boat down a placid river, his gaze fixed on a shimmering alabaster castle that lies ahead in the distance. Alas, this structure is a castle in the clouds, an insubstantial optical illusion. The river does not go to this castle; instead, in a feature the boy does not notice, the river takes a sharp turn and plunges down steep rapids. One can hardly imagine a starker contrast: the glowing future that the young sailor in his naive self-confidence expects versus the grim reality that actually awaits him.

The same kind of contrast between hopes and reality overtook the early movements of reform. In the grip of simplistic beliefs about government, the activists had the highest hopes. Alas, the

shimmering alabaster city was an illusion: the ideal of a fair, prosperous, happy society managed by government was a destination
logically impossible to reach. As the country drags its way toward
the bitter end of the experiment with big government, the appeal
of this image has faded. Yet the illusions that gave rise to it are
still at work in our politics today, preventing well-intentioned
idealists from turning away from the big government they keep
deploring.

To a large extent, this book tracks my own intellectual journey,
for I began my career as a political scientist in the grip of the illusions discussed in the following pages, and I had very high expec-
tations about what government can accomplish. Perhaps clever
people knew about these fallacies, but my teachers did not bring
them to my attention. It took decades of research and reflection
on my own to recognize these everyday errors and to realize how
deeply they were embedded in my thinking.

It's true: the really important ideas about government I
learned after I got my Ph.D. in political science. That's embarrassing for me to have to admit—and perhaps also an embarrassing
reflection on my graduate school—but what's important is to get
these elementary fallacies recognized so that future generations of
students and would-be reformers will be aware of them.

1

The Philanthropic Illusion

"He Has a Thousand Dollars!"

The financial system of modern government is staggeringly complicated. It imposes scores of taxes that create direct and indirect burdens on hundreds of millions of taxpaying individuals and organizations, and it has thousands of different kinds of benefits that it gives to those same hundreds of millions. If anyone were to attempt to draw up a chart of all the connections in government's tax-and-spend arrangements he would need a sheet of paper larger than an Idaho county, and he would not finish drafting even a corner of this chart in his lifetime.

Because we cannot grasp government's financial system in all its complexity, we reach for analogies or simplifications based on obvious features. The first feature one is apt to notice about government is that it has money—lots of it. Government seems to be a fabulously wealthy entity that can—if its heart is in the right place—shower wealth on worthy causes and needy individuals. Years ago, when my daughter Ellen was five and just

11

beginning to grasp the meaning of the word *money,* I asked her, "Ellen, should the government give money to poor people who don't have any?"

She thought very hard about this as she tried to fit novel concepts together. Her eyes finally lit up as an answer clicked into place. "Yes," she exclaimed, "because he has a thousand dollars!"

She saw government as a fabulously wealthy person ($1,000 was the largest sum she could imagine), and, applying the principle of sharing that she had been taught, she reasoned that "he" should therefore share his excess wealth with the less fortunate. Ellen was a victim of the *philanthropic illusion: the idea that government has money of its own.* Those who accept this premise will consider government payments to nice-seeming causes helpful. If you ask them whether government should promote the arts or help education or support science, their answer will be an unhesitating "yes."

The problem is that government does not have any money of its own. Any money that it has to spend has first to be taken away from a nation's citizens, and this process of taking injures the people and the activities forced to give up the funds. Government taxation takes money away from the arts, away from education, and away from science. Once you realize that government's giving has to be counterbalanced by taking, you become much less enthusiastic about government spending programs.

I believe that when most young people first contemplate the political realm, they begin with Ellen's perspective of government as a generous philanthropist capable of helping good causes and needy individuals. As they mature, this perspective becomes overlain by more sophisticated ideas. They notice that government raises money through taxes, and they become aware that they pay taxes. For many people, however, the philanthropic illusion is not fully overcome and consciously discarded. It remains lodged in their thinking, giving them a falsely positive view of government spending programs.

A number of complexities and confusions concerning government finance keep many people from clearly grasping the connection between government's nice-seeming giving and its harmful taking. One problem is that most people are not aware of the full burden of taxation as it falls on them and on causes they consider worthy. There are many different taxes, and most of them are paid in small and often unnoticeable ways. The telephone tax, for example, just seems to be a part of the phone bill. A gasoline tax is part of the cost of filling up. A sales tax on purchases is either unnoticed or seems small in most instances. The wage tax (Social Security and Medicare) is made to seem half as large as it actually is by having employers appear to pay half of it. Also, the use of the tax withholding system reduces the awareness of income tax payments.

Furthermore, much of the burden of taxes is born indirectly: it is passed on to someone else in the form of a higher price. For example, when a business pays the telephone tax, that amount simply becomes an expense to be passed along to consumers in higher prices. The property tax is shifted into rents. A person who does not own property still pays the property tax: it enters as a cost factored into his rent payment.

Corporation taxes, imposed by both the federal government and state governments, are perhaps the most poorly understood levies. The public believes that they are being paid by distant, impersonal entities and therefore assumes that these taxes do no harm to ordinary people. In fact, a corporation is a legal fiction, and all taxes levied on it must be borne by the human beings connected with the corporation. The burden of the corporation tax is shifted to its customers in the form of higher prices for the product the corporation produces, to its workers in the form of lower wages than they would otherwise have, and to its stockholders in the form of lower returns than would otherwise occur.

Because of the complexity and obscurity of taxes, most people do not have a clear idea of the total amount of money government is taking away from them. When they get a check from the government, they believe they have benefited and praise government for its intelligent generosity. They are not aware that in a thousand unnoticed ways they may have sent ten times that amount to the government in taxes. The situation is not unlike a stealthy cat burglar who sneaks into your bedroom and extracts bills from your wallet. He is careful not to take so much that you clearly notice the loss, and on the first Sunday of each month he comes to your door and gives some of the money back to you. You thank him for his generosity, and tell your neighbors that the world would be a better place if there were more people like him.

Some people disguise the philanthropic illusion through subjective perceptions of government's burdens. Because government's direct and indirect financial burdens are so difficult to grasp, the confusion allows observers to assume that government takes money only from people who don't need it or who don't deserve it. Some years ago, I interviewed a number of congressmen about fiscal policy, asking each one whether he was aware that the taxation to raise money for the spending programs he favored might be harming the very citizens he was trying to help. Not one of them could face this possibility. Congressman Joe Skeen, Republican from New Mexico, gave a typical answer:

> Q: How do you answer the point that even in the case of worthwhile programs, the money for them is being taken away from other people who had other uses for it?
> CONGRESSMAN SKEEN: Who are they?
>
> Q: Maybe they even wanted to feed their families, you could say? *(Congressman looks puzzled)* I mean, as taxpayers?
> CONGRESSMAN SKEEN: *(Flustered)* The effective level of removal from that area . . . there is nothing . . . if it were threatening the food, the clothing, the shelter areas, I would say that *any* government expenditure would be under serious scrutiny. But it doesn't affect that level.

Skeen had apparently never seriously considered that the taxation to pay for spending programs might do significant harm. When presented with this idea, he rejected it on the entirely subjective assumption that needy people don't bear any of the burden of taxation. This assumption is silly. It is a mathematical certainty that people deemed in need of food, clothing, and shelter are having money taken away from them through the direct and indirect operation of the tax system to the tune of thousands of dollars a year. What Skeen ought to have said is, "Yes, I know we're taking money away from them, but I hope we're giving them back more than we are taking away."

It is wrong, therefore, to view government services, payments, and subsidies as simple benefits that make a country a better place. One has to factor in the harm inflicted by raising the funds to pay for those benefits. Taxes drain resources from idealistic charities, innovative companies, educational institutions, art galleries, book publishers, and practically every other worthwhile human activity. Government takes money away from the poor it claims to feel sorry for. A study of minimum-wage workers in Portland, Oregon, found that the direct and indirect burden of taxes on these workers was $3,905 per year, or 40 percent of their total effective income.

Painter Donald Baechler is a prosperous, highly regarded artist who sells several hundred thousand dollars of his art around the world each year. In 1989, government officials decided he deserved a $15,000 subsidy from the National Endowment for the Arts (NEA), the idea being to "help" art. Unfortunately, this money didn't come from the sky. Baechler commented to the *Wall Street Journal,* "I paid about a quarter of my taxes with my NEA grant." So, with one hand government helped Baechler with its arts subsidy, and then with the other it turned around and took four times as much money away.

Commentators in the media reinforce the philanthropic illusion by the way they report on government spending programs. Reporters seldom connect the presumed good of a spending program with the actual harm inflicted by taking money away from people to pay for it. The politician who urges more spending on social programs is called "compassionate," whereas the politician who opposes this spending is called "heartless." A reporter who transcends the philanthropic illusion could point out that the lawmaker who opposed the subsidy is defending all the artists, poor people, homeowners, and so on who would be forced to pay taxes for the program.

Fairy tales about kings and queens encourage the illusion of free government wealth. Consider King Wenceslas, the "good" king in the popular Christmas carol who "looked out on the feast of Stephen" and saw an impoverished peasant. Wenceslas and his page took food to the peasant, and for his benevolence, the king acquired such a heated aura of saintliness that his footsteps melted snow! It is eloquent testimony to the strength of the philanthropic illusion that no one asks the critical question about King Wenceslas: Where did he get what he gave away? Everyone seems content to assume that he gave away his personal property.

If the king had been an ordinary person, working as a farmer or a woodcutter to earn his money, then giving alms would indeed have been an act of generosity. But kings do not get their wealth by selling something of value. What supports a monarch and his castles, stables, banquets, and page boys is taxes. Kings send their soldiers around to farms to force the peasants to give up chickens, corn, and cattle. Indeed, the peasant whom the king saw that night had probably been impoverished by the king's own taxation! So Wenceslas was just giving back a portion of what he had already taken away. Yet our culture immortalizes him in a holiday song that makes him a saint of compassion.

Faulty Economic Theories

Two of the most commonly heard arguments in support of government spending programs are outgrowths of the philanthropic illusion: that spending "puts money in circulation" and that it "creates jobs." Both are fallacious because they assume a source of wealth outside the economy. Whatever money the government "puts in circulation" by spending on goods and services is at the same time taken out of circulation through taxation.

The same point applies to job creation. Politicians often justify spending on attractive-sounding causes—spending for the arts, spending for school construction, spending for green energy— on the grounds that this spending will increase employment and help the economy. Such arguments are spurious. When the government creates jobs by hiring people, it does so by taking money away from people who would have created jobs by their own spending. The tax money that the entrepreneur sends to government would have been spent hiring workers to build a new factory. The tax money taken away from the consumer would have been spent paying workers to supply goods and services. Thus, there is no net increase in employment from the government tax-and-spend employment program.

There is the possibility, of course, that government might spend money it doesn't have. This process is known as deficit financing, and it might seem at first glance to be a way of assisting subsidy recipients without taking anything away from anybody else. A closer look reveals that this interpretation is groundless. There are only two ways government can spend money it hasn't taken away from the public in taxes: (1) it can borrow money, or (2) it can expand the money supply—that is, it can print money. Both methods simply shift the sacrifice the public has to make. If government borrows the funds, these funds must be repaid, with interest, by money raised from taxes levied on the public. If government prints money (or expands the money supply in any other way), it lowers the value of the money in the public's hands. With the extra government currency, there are now more dollars chasing the same amount of goods and services. These extra dollars will bid up prices so that people are able to buy fewer goods and services with the dollars they hold. In this way, when government makes purchases with newly printed money, it creates an "inflation tax" on the public.

The country has been experiencing this inflation tax for many years as the government has continually expanded the money supply to help pay its bills. When I was a boy, a candy bar cost five cents; today I have to pay a dollar for one. That's one of the things that happens when politicians assume they can help some people without hurting anyone else.

Seduced by Semantics

Americans seem to love subsidies, viewing government handouts in their many shapes and forms as natural and necessary: payments for the poor, payments for the middle class, payments for college students, apple growers, cotton farmers, and even the Polynesian Voyaging Society of Honolulu, Hawaii. If we do not have programs to subsidize viola playing, Morse code, or argyle socks, it's not because the public thinks they would be wrong, illogical, or destructive. We just haven't gotten around to them.

How did America become a subsidy-loving nation? The country obviously succumbed to the philanthropic illusion—the idea that government funds come from the sky. To a large extent, this illusion has been fostered by semantic techniques. The politicians developed a vocabulary that made the system of robbing Peter to pay Paul—and even the absurdity of robbing Peter to pay Peter—seem sensible and socially responsible.

The grandfather of the practice of semantic confusion was Franklin D. Roosevelt, and the textbook example of his craft was the Social Security program adopted in 1935. Roosevelt's idea was to force the entire country—poor, middle class, and wealthy—into a comprehensive national pension system. A new wage tax was begun, but it wasn't called a tax, but rather a "contribution," and the subsidy was not called a subsidy, but instead "social insurance." The deceptive marketing of Social Security was quite deliberate, as Arthur Altmeyer, Roosevelt confidante and first Social Security commissioner, said: "Every effort was made to use terminology that would inspire confidence rather than arouse suspicion." The funds that came in from the wage tax were described as going to "trust funds" in order to dupe the public into believing that these dollars were kept in specific piles in the Treasury to pay Social Security benefits. To further the illusion that workers are paying their own way, the Social Security Administration keeps records of each worker's "contributions," as if these tax payments establish a legal right to specific benefits. In reality, Social Security is simply a welfare program. Congress changes benefits whenever it wants, and the Supreme Court has declared (in *Nestor v. Fleming,* 363 U.S. 603 [1960]) that making Social Security tax payments gives no legal rights to benefits.

The Roosevelt administration's con job succeeded, and it gave birth to *entitlements,* a term that entered the language in 1944. Today, seniors both rich and poor calmly cash their Social Security checks, never pausing to notice that they are a government subsidy. "But I paid taxes into the program!" they say. But if paying some taxes entitles a person to a government payment, then everyone in America is entitled to every conceivable subsidy. Although the first recipient, Ida May Fuller, had paid only $25 in Social Security taxes, she collected benefits totaling $22,889. She became the poster girl for the program, not the least bit embarrassed by her staggering bonanza.

The politicians aren't the only ones using language to spin away economic realities and foster the philanthropic illusion. Government agencies do it too. If an agency's task is to give away taxpayer funds, doing a good job means giving out more money. The greatest nightmare for an administrator of the National Widget Assistance Program would be a small and declining number of people taking free widgets. To prevent this kind of disappointment, government agencies have copied Madison Avenue's advertising techniques and its abuse of language in selling their subsidies to the public.

The Food and Nutrition Service, the agency in charge of food stamps, exemplifies this pattern. It has a huge marketing and advertising program—which it euphemistically calls "outreach"—designed to boost food stamp use. The key to the marketing campaign is to inculcate the philanthropic illusion—that is, to fuzz over the reality that the recipient of the food subsidy is taking wealth from someone else.

One office in Pennsylvania sent a circular to a targeted group that began with this sentence: "With the rising cost of food, we wondered if you could use a little help at the grocery store." Maryland officials set up toll-free numbers, touch-screen computers in shopping malls, and a special card that "looks like a credit card, and therefore no one knows he [sic] is using food stamp benefits." In West Virginia, officials set up "outstations" in senior centers to facilitate applications and to reduce the "welfare office stigma." To motivate the development of innovative marketing tactics, the Food and Nutrition Service has a "Hunger Heroes" award program for officials who provide "exemplary service in assisting eligible clients obtain food stamps."

The Food and Nutrition Service conducted market research to find out why more people weren't signing up for food stamps. The answer, the researchers found, is pride. As one interviewee put it, "Well, I was from the generation where no way did you take that stuff. You either worked for it or you did without."

You and I may think that the disposition not to mooch off others is a healthy social attitude, but officials in subsidy programs abhor it. After all, this honorable outlook blocks expansion of their programs. So these officials have developed marketing materials to make the public feel that when it comes to taking government benefits, "there's no need to be ashamed of it," as one official put it. They have worked to break down recipients' reluctance to accept subsidies and have substituted reassuring slogans that present benefit programs as "rights," philanthropic "help" to which recipients are "legally entitled."

The use of the word *government* in connection with spending programs encourages the acceptance of the philanthropic illusion. To be rigorous, we should describe a spending program as a relationship between those who give up funds and those who get them. The entity managing this exchange, government, should be off to one side. Unfortunately, government typically becomes the object of our attention, so we personify it as if it were an independent source of wealth.

Consider this statement by columnist Harold Myerson, writing in the *Washington Post* on September 8, 2004: "At a time when private employers everywhere are cutting back on health insurance and shunning defined-benefit pensions, government can move in to fill the gap." At first, this sounds like a compassionate, constructive policy suggestion. But remember, government isn't a philanthropist. It doesn't have any funds of its own. It's just a system of extracting and distributing funds. If we rephrase the policy advice to drop the word *government* and focus instead on the transfer of wealth, it looks like this: "At a time when private employers everywhere are cutting back on health insurance and shunning defined-benefit pensions, money should be taken from some people and given to others or back to the same people in the form of health care and pensions." The policy proposal is thus exposed as circular nonsense.

The use of the word *government* as the provider of funds, goods, or services is a shorthand we all use; nevertheless, it incorporates the philanthropic illusion and thus encourages listeners to suppose that government has funds of its own.

Human images are sometimes substituted for the term *government*, a sure sign of the philanthropic illusion. On October 26, 2004 another *Washington Post* columnist, Abigail Trafford, devoted an entire article to praising Medicare. She quoted a senior citizen, Ann Satterthwaite, who was highly pleased with the Medicare program: "It's a comforting feeling knowing that Uncle Sam is there," Satterthwaite said. "I'm very grateful." Trafford did not present the remark as a fallacy. She endorsed it! Correctly rephrased to avoid the philanthropic illusion, Satterthwaite's comment should have been, "It's a comforting feeling knowing that money will be taken away from other people to pay my medical bills."

A Visit to the "Love Your Neighbor" Committee

Politicians are especially likely to fall victim to the philanthropic illusion given the nature of their role in the system. They are surrounded by claimants who are begging for funds, urging them to give to needy people and worthy causes. After the politicians do make the appropriation, the supplicants express gratitude. "Thank you for your help," they say. It's not surprising that these public officials come to think of themselves as philanthropists and forget all about the people they are taking money away from to pay for the program.

The transcripts of congressional committee hearings contain many examples of this one-sided thinking. In 2001, the chairman of a House appropriations subcommittee, Republican Ralph Regula from Ohio, was introducing the principal witness, Secretary of Health and Human Services Tommy Thompson. Here were his words: "I've said this before—the Bible says there's two great commandments. One is to love the Lord and the second is to love your neighbor. We're the 'Love Your Neighbor Committee,' and you're the 'Love Your Neighbor Secretary' because there isn't a person in America that's not touched in some way or another by what you're doing in that agency."

In his reply, Thompson embraced this perspective: "It truly is love your neighbor. This Department, as you know, Chairman, actually interacts with every American. Every man, woman and child somehow is affected by the Department of Health and Human Services budget. So it is an awesome responsibility that I have and that you have. Together, with bipartisanship, I think we do a great job and leave a great legacy and help a lot of Americans improve their quality of life."

Notice the view of government finances revealed in these statements. Both men are speaking as though government were a source of wealth, as though it were a philanthropist with excess money to give away to good causes. Indeed, they feel that in doling out this wealth, they themselves are the philanthropists. This view is false. The money that Regula is appropriating is not his.

He did not earn it, and he does not possess it. He is not showing generosity in giving these funds to agencies, programs, and beneficiaries. He is just a middleman in a process of distribution. He is not one penny poorer as a result of the distribution. The people who are made poorer are the taxpayers.

Imagine what would happen to government officials' perspective if they were surrounded by taxpayers who were conscious of and articulate about the specific injuries that the tax-and-spend system was inflicting on them. Parents would explain how taxes lowered their income and made it impossible to send their children to college. Young adults would explain how taxation took money away from them so they couldn't properly care for ailing parents. Entrepreneurs would complain that they couldn't start businesses and create jobs because the money to do so has been taken away by taxation. Over the years, Regula and Thompson would begin to grasp the elementary truth that a government spending program is like a seesaw. The money to "improve the quality of life" for some people is taken away from other people, *thus impairing their quality of life*. Regula would discover that he is chairing the Love *and Hurt* Your Neighbor Committee.

A lawmaker liberated from the philanthropic illusion would describe his difficult balancing task this way: "Mr. Secretary, we know you have been working hard to put a good face on your programs. These programs may do some good, but they certainly do harm as well because they take money away from all Americans, including the poorest of the poor. It is our responsibility to make sure that the value of these programs more than outweighs the enormous sacrifices they entail."

Most lawmakers abhor such frank language, for it deflates their self-image as generous saviors of the people. Here's another example of this mentality, from the *Congressional Record* for 1984. In paying tribute to a deceased Pennsylvania lawmaker, Democratic Congressman Robert Young of Missouri stated, "William Barrett was a man who always served the people, and his long record in this body indicates clearly the contribution he made for people in the fields of social welfare, housing, and urban development. He worked hard and successfully to use the vast resources of the Federal Government to serve the most in need and to correct injustice."

Congressman Young was laboring under an illusion. The federal government doesn't have "vast resources." What it has is vast power, in the form of the tax system, to take resources away from the American people. But this eulogy would not be offering much praise if it recognized this elementary truth and stated that the deceased congressman worked "hard and successfully to take money away from taxpayers and give it to others."

When Subsidies Are Justified

The preceding discussion should not be taken as a blanket condemnation of subsidies. The argument here is not that a subsidy is necessarily wrong, but that most people defend subsidies on a fallacious basis. They presume that the money being spent is "free;" that is, they overlook the harm and suffering that government inflicts by taking the money away to pay for the subsidy. Seen through the rose-colored glasses of the philanthropic illusion, subsidies appear much more attractive to them than they should.

The correct way to defend a subsidy is to try to make a full and accurate accounting of the harm caused by raising the money for it. If one feels sorry for farmers whose crops have failed and wishes to propose a subsidy to help them, one needs to detail where the money is coming from and what harm this taxation will do. For example, some of the money for the farm subsidy will come from art museums, so that their mission will be impaired. Perhaps the tax will add to the museums' wage bills or to their construction costs; perhaps the tax will take money away from prospective donors, so they won't contribute as much; and so on. Once this harm is identified, the backer of the subsidy can say he feels that the help for farmers outweighs the harm to art museums. This assessment is a value judgment he is entitled to make.

In principle, the backer of the subsidy should go on to detail all the other entities that will be harmed, but this kind of detailed accounting is beyond anyone's ability. An acceptable oversimplification is to say, "I want to help farmers at the expense of every other needy person and every other good cause in the country." This is the honest way to defend a subsidy.

This example assumes that there are only a few subsidies. Subsidies become much more questionable when there is a large number of them, because the system runs up against a mathematical limitation. Assume a country where government gives subsidies to every population group. If the tax burden and subsidy level is equal for all, there can be no benefit for any group: the amount each gains in subsidy is lost through taxation to pay for the subsidies for all the others. The entire subsidy system is a waste of effort. When we add the point that the subsidies introduce economic inefficiency—an issue discussed in chapter 3—then everyone loses in this situation of multiple subsidies. All citizens are poorer than they would be if there were no subsidies. The conclusion, then, is that *as the number and size of subsidies increases, government spending programs become increasingly destructive for all beneficiaries.* It is therefore irresponsible to propose more subsidies in a system already heavily laden with subsidies.

Modern politicians fail to grasp this point. Laboring under the philanthropic illusion, they assume that government can always spend more for some good purpose. The result of this approach is a vast vicious cycle of multiple subsidies. Government taxes homeowners to provide assistance for farmers, then taxes hospital patients to provide assistance to homeowners, and then taxes farmers to provide assistance for hospital patients, and so forth. This arrangement is not only economically self-defeating, but socially unhealthy as well. It invites everyone to try to live at the expense of everyone else by engaging in lobbying and political agitation.

The attraction of government spending is at the bottom of the economic malaise found all around the world, from Kenya to Venezuela, from Athens to Detroit. In the grip of the philanthropic illusion, politicians and the public are treating government as a benevolent source of funds. We need to stop using euphemisms such as "Farmers need more help" or "Government should encourage science." Instead, we should accurately describe the policy we are proposing: "People should be required to give more money to farmers;" "People should be required to give more money to scientists." This kind of honesty in public discourse would shatter the philanthropic illusion that fosters the unhealthy modern system of reciprocal plunder.

2

The Voluntary Illusion

Franz Kafka, Call Your Office!

Browsing the Internal Revenue Service (IRS) Web site one day not long ago, I discovered a quiz prepared and posted by the IRS chief counsel's office. It was an interactive test, and you could keep taking it without penalty until you got it right—a rather remarkable departure from the usual way the IRS operates! Here were the questions:

1. I don't have to pay taxes because payment is voluntary.
   o true   o false

2. The government has the right to force me to pay my taxes and charge me penalties for not paying taxes.
   o true   o false

3. IRS publications state that the tax system is voluntary.
   o true   o false

The Web site says that the correct answer to the first question is "false." Payment of taxes is *not* voluntary. The correct answer to the second question is "true": the government *does* have the right to force you to pay your taxes. With these answers under your belt, you figure the third one should be a snap. You mark "false," only to discover you are dead wrong! The correct answer is "true." IRS publications do indeed say that the tax system is voluntary.

In the 1920s, Czech writer Franz Kafka created stories about the way bureaucracies make bizarre and contradictory demands—thus giving us the adjective *Kafkaesque* to refer to such absurdities. Kafka's stories were fiction, but I'm afraid he has been outdone in this real-world example produced by the IRS chief counsel. Here is a scene for a drama modeled after Kafka's *The Trial:*

> EXAMINER: The tax system is voluntary, isn't it?
> PRISONER: *(frightened, insecure, taking his cue from the examiner)* Uh, yes, sir.
> EXAMINER: *(slaps prisoner's face)* No, you fool! That's the wrong answer! Now try again. How do you describe our voluntary tax system in the United States?
> PRISONER: *(conflicted, looking left and right, speaking with caution)* Uh . . . it's . . . not voluntary?
> EXAMINER: Well done! *(to the guard)* Release the prisoner!

Bureaucratic absurdities have their source in logically inconsistent political demands. IRS documents do indeed say, in hundreds of places, that the tax system is "voluntary." Some citizens take these statements at face value and refuse to pay taxes on the grounds that they would rather not. The chief counsel explains the resulting problem: "Some assert that they are not required to file federal tax returns because the filing of a tax return is voluntary. Proponents point to the fact that the IRS itself tells taxpayers in the Form 1040 instruction book that the tax system is voluntary. Additionally, the Supreme Court's opinion in *Flora v. United States,* 362 U.S. 145, 176 (1960), is often quoted for the proposition that 'our system of taxation is based upon voluntary assessment and payment, not upon distraint.'"

The contradictory quiz was the chief counsel's effort to warn people away from thinking the tax system is voluntary just because the IRS and the Supreme Court say it is. That leaves unanswered the larger question: Why does the IRS say the tax system is voluntary? The answer is the *voluntary illusion: the impulse to want to believe that government action is not based on the use of force.* Let's explore how this illusion comes about.

Government is based on physical force. This is not to say that force is the only reason people obey government. Citizens may follow its commands because they feel the commands are sensible, because they respect officials, because they feel proud of their country, and so on. The critical point is what happens to those who *don't* want to do what government wants. Those who doubt that government is based on force should try disobeying even the simplest of government's commands. Try not paying a parking fine, for example. You will first get letters saying you must pay the amount; then you will get letters saying you must pay double the original amount; and one day you find a clamp has been placed on the tire of your car. You get a power hacksaw and begin to cut away this offensive clamp, and a policeman comes along and tells you to stop. You tell him to mind his own business. He seizes you,

you pull away, he shoves you to the ground and pins your hands behind your back with handcuffs. That's physical force.

In another jurisdiction, authorities may not use a wheel clamp. Ignore all their letters and a document will come saying you have to appear in court. Ignore that, and another document will say you are in contempt of court. Keep tearing up these missives, treating them as if they were junk mail from a giant corporation, and you will discover the ultimate difference between a corporation and a government. A government sends police officers to surround your house and to ask you to leave because you no longer own it, the deed having been transferred to another party to pay the contempt of court fine. You say your home is your castle, and you brandish a shotgun to defend your property. A policeman shoots you, and whether the subsequent tribunal later decides he acted rightly or not quite rightly, you are still dead. That's physical force.

"Political power grows out of the barrel of a gun," said Communist Chinese dictator Mao Zedong. His maxim rather grates on Western ears, for it contradicts the ideal of a politics based on understanding and reason, but it contains an earthy truth: physical force does lie at the bottom of politics. Of course, there are differences between regimes in the amount of force being used. In the more civilized nations, government refrains from using force to suppress the expression of opinions: freedom of speech, we call it. And in these more civilized places, government applies force rather patiently, sending lots of letters announcing doubled and redoubled fines before it sends the police. If you failed to pay one of Mao's parking tickets, your body might be thrown into the river the next day. So there are important differences of degree in the application of force from one system to another.

There is also an important distinction to be made in how government's force is used. Throughout history, it has generally been agreed that there must be some entity to react to the violence initiated by individuals. Murderers, robbers, rapists need to be caught and punished, and doing so generally requires the use of force. This *reactive* use of force is government's first function. If government did not punish and deter the violent behavior of gangs and individuals, a society might well descend into anarchy or, as philosopher Thomas Hobbes put it, into a "war of all against all."

This *reactive* use of force needs to be distinguished from the *assertive* use of force, the situation when government agents initiate the use of force. When philosophers and activists advocate using government to fix problems and create a fairer society, it is this assertive use of force to which they appeal. They want government to go beyond the job of restraining violence. They want government agents to initiate the use of force against peaceful individuals, to compel them to do something they would not otherwise do. For example, taxation means that government agents initiate force against those who decline to "donate" to the government. Prohibiting marijuana means that government agents initiate force against peaceful individuals who are growing or selling this crop.

One can debate whether one or another of these assertive uses of force is wise or effective. One can argue that it is right to arrest tax evaders and wrong to arrest marijuana growers—or vice versa. This is not the place to explore such policy issues. I am simply pointing out that the policies of modern big government assume that it is right for government agents to initiate force against peaceful individuals.

Centuries ago, when violence was more common and more accepted than it is today, the observation that government power is based on the assertive use of force would have raised no eyebrows. That government officials used physical force to impose their will on peaceful individuals was an obvious, everyday occurrence. When Puritan journalist John Stubbs wrote a pamphlet advising Queen Elizabeth not to marry a French Catholic prince, Elizabeth and her ministers had the public executioner cut off his right hand. Stubbs, knowing that he stood within an inch of losing his head, raised the bloody stump of his right hand after the mutilation and shouted, "Long live the Queen!" If someone had asked Stubbs, "Is government based on force?" he would have said, "Duh!"

As I have explained in my book *A History of Force* (2004), the world has been experiencing a broad evolution against the use of physical force. This evolution has been reflected both in a decline in coercive practices (we don't cut off offending writers' hands any more) and in changing attitudes. The prevailing view in more advanced cultures is that force is a primitive, even barbaric, approach. Many of the more socially aware people don't believe even in spanking children.

This distaste toward force today creates a powerful psychological pressure to repress the recognition of government's coercive nature. Cultured, socially responsible people are loath to admit that the money for the subsidized opera they have just enjoyed was raised at the point of bayonets. They want to believe that the government in which they place their trust operates on sensitive, high-minded principles. This need to repress the ugly side of government's action is the basis of the voluntary illusion.

You can test the power of this illusion by asking your friends and neighbors the simple question, "Is government based on force?" Many people will flatly say, "No." Many others will exhibit evasion, confusion, or embarrassment—all a product of the voluntary illusion. The answer given by my friend Nancy is typical: "Well, it shouldn't be." Then she added, "I suppose that's dodging the question."

It's not hard to read Nancy's thinking. She knows in one corner of her mind that government is based on force, which she deplores. Yet she looks to government to fix society's problems. She feels that Social Security, Medicare, food stamps, public education, and so on, are desirable programs. Hence, she is conflicted. She doesn't want to disparage the big government she likes by recognizing its distasteful foundation in brute physical force.

Now we can understand why IRS officials—and judges and congressmen—feel the need to say that the U.S. tax system is voluntary when it isn't: they are uneasy about taxation's use of force. After all, consider what's involved. IRS officials send millions of enforcement letters to citizens every year, threatening to send armed agents to seize homes, cars, businesses, paychecks, and savings. These citizens have not attacked anyone or stolen from anyone. They have peacefully gone about their business and earned a living. It is government that is initiating force against them to take away their money. These collection actions are extremely stressful for the people involved—sometimes more stressful, from their point of view, than a robbery. IRS enforcement actions lead to destroyed businesses, homelessness, broken marriages, mental illness, and suicide.

This is not to say IRS officials are wrong to engage in these harsh practices. This is what a system of collecting money from people by force entails. But it *is* an ugly system, and it taints those associated with it. When we are making a list of charming, sympathetic people to invite to our party, the names of IRS collection officers do not leap to mind.

IRS officials sense the taint, and it creates a powerful subconscious urge to blot out this disreputable feature of their activity. When leaving for work in the morning, they cannot say to their spouses, "Bye-bye, honey. I'm off to take some more money from people by force." That is why they want to say (and why IRS publications actually state) that their coercive system is "voluntary."

One respondent in my survey, George, gave a nontypical response to my question "Is government based on force?" "Absolutely!" he replied without hesitation. Unlike Nancy, George is a crusty libertarian who feels most government subsidy programs are mistaken. He illustrates the point that those who openly recognize government's coercive nature are less likely to favor big government.

No Force in Utopia

In January 1888, the son of a Baptist minister from Chicopee, Massachusetts, gave the world an unusual novel. It wasn't a particularly good novel. The writing style was pedantic, the plot almost nonexistent, and the characters wooden puppets speaking the author's proclamations. Nevertheless, this book hit a publishing jackpot, selling more than two hundred thousand copies in its first year and passing the half-million mark within a few years.

Edward Bellamy's *Looking Backward* was not, in truth, a novel at all. It was a treatise on political philosophy disguised as fiction. The reason for its great sales was that intellectuals across the country found its political vision immensely attractive. The hero of the novel, Julian West, living in Boston in 1887, falls asleep and wakes up in the year 2000 to discover that government has eliminated poverty, suffering, and injustice. The "story" consists of Julian asking questions about how this utopia works and listening to the answers. (The book does include a slight love interest. Julian had a girlfriend in Boston, whom he necessarily lost by rudely going to sleep for 113 years, but he meets her direct descendant and spitting image in the new utopia. Thus, Bellamy took the old romantic formula and gave it a delightful new twist: boy meets girl, boy loses girl, boy gets great-granddaughter).

To modern eyes, the utopia that Bellamy promised is depressingly familiar, for we saw it attempted in dozens of twentieth-century Communist regimes. In Bellamy's United States of 2000, there is no private property. Government owns everything—land, factories, and houses—and it directs all production and provides all services. There is no gap between the rich and poor because the government gives everyone the same stipend, whatever work they do, whether they work or not.

The first real-world effort to create a government-based Communist utopia came in Russia in 1917, and the one thing we know about it and about numerous other Marxist regimes that came later is that establishing and maintaining this kind of arrangement requires an enormous use of force. People object to having the state take away their property, so regular police, secret police, and armies have to intimidate, imprison, and kill these opponents. Because people evade government economic requirements by selling on the black market, violence is needed to discourage this independence. People speak out against the regime's harshness and high-handedness, so the police crush freedom of speech, freedom of the press, and freedom of assembly. In practice, efforts to implement a socialist utopia through government have cost rivers of blood.

Bellamy's readers did not have the benefit of this hindsight, of course, but their common sense would have told them that the sweeping regimentation he envisioned would require a heavy coercive hand, a hand that would inflict pain and suffering on those who disagreed or resisted.

This commonsense objection gave Bellamy a problem: how to keep his sensitive, middle-class readers—who were forming "Bellamy clubs" by the score to implement his ideal—from being repelled by his utopia's coercive foundation. Bellamy solved his problem just like the IRS does, by saying (in the words of Doctor Leete, Julian's guide to this utopia), "Our system depends in no particular on legislation, *but is entirely voluntary,* the logical outcome of human nature under rational conditions" (italics added). Was there revolutionary upheaval or bloodshed when the sweeping regimentation was put in place? No, assures Leete, it came about with "absolutely no violence." When the time traveler asks what happened to the famous state penitentiary in Charleston, Massachusetts, Leete declares, "We have no jails nowadays."

Asserting that the system is voluntary certainly makes the utopia attractive to modern intellectuals, but one does have to wonder if it is realistic. For example, the novel declares that the state abolished all buying and selling as well as all kinds of money. Is it reasonable to suppose that no one, not one person out of scores of millions, would want to sell a ring or a watch? How would such an act be prevented in Bellamy's society unless it included policemen who arrested those making back-alley exchanges?

It seems Bellamy himself was aware of the unrealism of his scheme because at one point he contradicts himself about the use of force. It concerns the management of the "industrial army," the military-style organization into which all men ages twenty-one to forty-five are drafted to do the nation's labor. In the main, Bellamy describes this arrangement as one of gentle cooperation. The choice of jobs is "purely voluntary," and participation "is regarded as so absolutely natural and reasonable that the idea of its being compulsory has ceased to be thought of," says Leete. Yet at one point, harsh treatment is contemplated. Leete gets to the possibility of there being lazy workers: "As for the actual neglect of work, positively bad work, or other overt remissness on the part of men incapable of generous motives, the discipline of the industrial army is far too strict to allow anything whatever of that sort. A man able to duty, and persistently refusing, is sentenced to solitary imprisonment on bread and water till he consents." That statement flatly contradicts the claim that the utopia is "completely voluntary" with "no jails." Bellamy has admitted that occasionally there are lazy people and that the state must use physical force to compel them to cooperate.

It's a telling inconsistency. The voluntary illusion is never a thoroughgoing one. Those subject to it know, with one part of their minds, that government does use force. Their problem is that they cannot consistently and openly admit it. In order to make government seem more attractive than it is, they avoid mentioning its basis in coercion.

If Bellamy had not been subject to the voluntary illusion, he would have admitted the coercive foundation of his utopia from the outset. He would have suggested how many millions of police officers it had, how many jails, and how many prisoners languished in them. He would have conceded that great pain and suffering would be inflicted in trying to keep people in line. For example, a family would be broken up when the police drag a mother off to jail for selling her earrings.

Frankly recognizing the coercive basis of his utopia would not invalidate it, of course. Anyone is entitled to propose policies based on the application of physical force. Perhaps they are good policies, perhaps they are necessary ones, and perhaps they will make us happier in the long run. My point here is that those who advocate government schemes should not cover up or evade the aspect of force that these schemes entail, because pretending they are voluntary gives them a false attractiveness.

How to Fund an Orphanage

When people are asked if government is based on force, they sometimes answer that government's use of force—along with its armies, police, and prisons—is not "really" force. They see some special character about government that transmutes its violence into something else, something nicer that they can approve of. We can explore this issue with a hypothetical illustration.

You are Mother Francesca, head of an orphanage in a little town in Sicily. The orphanage was endowed by a nobleman a century ago and gets some voluntary donations from year to year. Nevertheless, its budget is tight, and you have to scrimp to make ends meet. You can't afford to keep the orphanage fully heated in the winter, and there isn't as much nutritious food as the children ought to have. Some of them get sick, and on occasion one dies, the death probably caused in part by the inadequate heating and poor diet.

One day the head of the local mafia, Don Alfonso, comes by and offers to raise money for the orphanage in the way he knows best. He will run a protection racket in town, threatening to kidnap store owners unless they each contribute 200 lira a month to the orphanage. With these sums coming in, you know you will be able to heat the orphanage and provide the children with nutritious food. When you seem undecided, Don Alfonso says, "Think of the children, Mama Francesca!"

Do you accept his offer?

Everyone I've given this problem to, including extremely compassionate individuals, says the don's offer should be refused. In other words, everyone agrees that it is wrong to rely on this kind of violence for a good cause.

Now suppose that Don Alfonso is appointed mayor of the village, and some of his mafia henchmen are named to the city council. He is a perfectly proper, legal government official now. He comes to you with a proposition: he and his council will approve a tax of 200 lira a month on store owners, the proceeds of which will go to the orphanage. The tax will be enforced by the police, who will drag to jail those shopkeepers who refuse to pay it—which is, of course, a legal kidnapping. Now what do you say to his proposal?

Perhaps you will agree. After all, using force legally is probably better than using it illegally. However, there's no getting around that it still is force.

In this example, Don Alfonso is appointed mayor, so he doesn't necessarily represent or speak for anyone in the village. Some would argue that this detail makes his use of force illegitimate. Well then, let's change the circumstances. Say Don Alfonso and his henchmen are voted into their offices in an election rather tainted by the typical shenanigans that mar most such contests. Perhaps Don Alfonso falsely accused his opponent of seducing a nun, or perhaps he outspent his opponent ten to one in campaign propaganda, but, anyway, there he is, the democratically elected mayor. Now what do you say to his offer?

As Mother Francesca, you are going to have to do a great deal of head scratching to decide if this "democratic" foundation of Don Alfonso's authority supplies a moral basis for accepting money raised through the threat of force. Life, you say with a sigh of irritation, was so much easier before the political scientist who pens this book came along and shattered the voluntary illusion.

Happy Family or Abusive Father?

Government programs are desirable, say some philosophers, because they implement community spirit. They say a nation is a social group whose members want to help each other, and government is the agency for implementing this spirit of generosity. Economist Arthur Benavie defends the Social Security program in these terms. "Society is a family responsible for its members," he writes, "Risks are shared. The cost of caring for the elderly and disabled is spread over the entire society."

The problem with all such analogies is that they incorporate the voluntary illusion: they forget about government's use of force. Society may be akin to a family, but government is not a benevolent father urging members to be generous toward each other. Its police officers and jails force people to be generous. In a healthy family, help is given voluntarily, motivated by love and respect. If there's a parallel between Social Security and a family, you have to ask what kind of family it is where dad gets his children to support him by pointing a shotgun at them. The answer: a dysfunctional and resentful one.

Swedish economist Assar Lindbeck adopts the same benevolent view as Benavie, arguing that welfare programs reflect a generous society caring for its members. He states, "I have often described the modern welfare state as 'a triumph of western civilization.'"

Let's look more closely at how the modern welfare state operates. It is indeed true that the impulse to take care of the needy has a generous origin and that many people pay taxes willingly as a reflection of their spirit of community. But many others do not feel so generous. They resist paying taxes, and they have to be coerced to comply with government's demands. Because of this resistance, the tax system has to treat everyone as a potential criminal. The result is an ever-growing system of surveillance and punishment. Employers and bankers are required to report every significant financial transaction to the IRS, which each year collects more than one billion pieces of financial information on citizens. The IRS assesses more than 30 million penalties each year against taxpayers who have failed to live up to its demands. To uphold the fear on which the tax system depends, the IRS sends hundreds of people to prison each year. Just as in totalitarian dictatorships, the IRS has cultivated a system of informers: it gives cash rewards to thousands of people who snitch on friends and family members. The entire system involves scores of thousands of pages of burdensome, confusing regulations that spawn millions of costly, frustrating disputes every year.

The sinister and frustrating features of the tax system might be excused if the welfare-giving side of the redistribution process were gracious and uplifting. Unfortunately, it too is frustrating and degrading. Although some welfare recipients are appreciative, many others aren't grateful to the "community" that has sacrificed to help them out. Instead, they are peeved that this community doesn't provide more help, and this attitude disposes them to cheat the system.

I became aware of this problem of dishonesty when I undertook a study of welfare systems some years ago (*Overcoming*

Welfare, 1998). In one study, carried out in 1988, researcher Kathryn Edin gained the confidence of twenty-five women receiving welfare benefits and was able to learn about their actual budgets in detail. She found that all twenty five had unreported income and were therefore cheating the system. Most had unreported full or part-time jobs; others were getting income from boyfriends and other family members. In the same year, a detailed IRS audit of the earned income tax credit, another welfare program, found that 42 percent of the recipients had misrepresented their status in order to obtain higher benefits.

The result of this disposition to evade welfare requirements is that the welfare office is the mirror image of the tax office. On the welfare agent's desk is a thick compendium of regulations that have grown in number and complexity beyond any human being's capacity to understand. Applicants for benefits must fill out lengthy forms documenting their claim to neediness. They are required to supply extensive personal information to enable bureaucrats to check up on them. Like the tax system, the welfare system tries to intimidate clients into telling the truth. In many places, welfare recipients are fingerprinted in an effort to control fraud. California has developed a "secret witness program," a system of informers who are rewarded for turning in friends and relatives for welfare violations. At a food stamps office in Sandpoint, Idaho, a poster on the wall says, "It's all plugged in," and lists some of the databases that the Welfare Department uses to check statements made on applications. In large type, it menacingly announces, "IF YOU DON'T TELL US, SOMEBODY ELSE WILL."

The problem with the welfare state lies not in the basic concept of sharing. Equality is a noble social goal that, when pursued through voluntary means, enhances the spirit of community and strengthens the bonds between individuals. Wealthier parents assist poorer children; wealthier children assist poorer parents. Richer friends pick up the tab for poorer friends. Better-off professionals shade their bills for clients who are less well off. Philanthropists endow public facilities that the poor may use at below cost or at no cost. Wealthier individuals sustain voluntary groups, such as churches and Boy Scouts, from which the less fortunate benefit. All are positive, commendable acts of voluntary income redistribution.

When force is used to implement equality, however, the ideal turns sour. Both donors and recipients wind up ensnared in a Big Brother apparatus of surveillance and control that assumes that everyone is trying to cheat everyone else.

This ugly reality eluded Professor Lindbeck, I suspect, because his thinking was clouded by the voluntary illusion. He vaguely assumed that the welfare state's transactions are based on gentle cooperation. Correct this assumption and his statement should look like this: "The modern welfare state, which employs force and the threat of force to try to redistribute income, is a triumph of Western civilization." Now the claim looks unappealing, if not downright bizarre.

The cause of honest, constructive social philosophy would be much advanced if activists and politicians would explicitly recognize the state's foundation in physical force. They need to state frankly whether they are willing to have government agents imprison or even kill people in order to make their policies work. If they are not, then they probably shouldn't be looking to government to accomplish their goals.

3

The Illusion of the Frictionless State

How High Can a Concrete Airplane Fly?

The human mind has great powers of abstraction. We look at the earth, with its oceans, mountains, turtles, and butterflies, and say it is, simply, a sphere. We see a freight train with its thundering engines and carloads of plywood, coal, and ethyl acetate and describe it as a simple mass of so many thousand tons.

In most fields, this technique of oversimplification does not cause problems because we know we are doing it, and we are careful to reintroduce complexities as we move to the real-world applications of our ideas. In physics, for example, we calculate how much energy resides in a barrel of oil, and, by making oversimplifications, we can calculate how far this energy will propel a truck up a hill. We hastily add that we are speaking "theoretically." We know that when we move to the real world, we will have to reintroduce the complexities that we set aside. These complexities show up as *friction:* the waste, losses, and inefficiency in the systems of transmitting energy from one form to another. We know

47

that once we include the inefficiencies, obstacles, and imperfec-
tions of real-world systems, the truck's performance may be quite
disappointing.

When it comes to politics, the human mind does not function
in this sober, skeptical way. Even though the complexities involved
in government are vastly greater than in any purely physical system, humans are seldom capable of sensing the inefficiencies these
complexities bring to real-world applications. When we make a
statement such as "Government should provide shoes for poor
children," we do not add, "speaking theoretically." We assume that
our intention can be carried out without significant waste. We
do not imagine that the inefficiency in government's system of
trying to transfer wealth from some people and deliver it in the
form of shoes to poor children might entail costs so high that we
would choke in embarrassment if we learned of them. We do not
imagine that the waste might be so great that no shoes at all get
delivered! These skeptical thoughts don't trouble us because we
are victims of the *illusion of the frictionless state: the idea that the*
state can transfer resources with negligible overhead cost.

Over the years, perhaps the greatest victims of this illusion
have been scholars and philosophers. They are used to looking at
the world theoretically, as though a nation were a sandbox to be
rearranged according to a pleasing design and the government
were the supremely powerful agent who can do the rearrang-
ing. The philosopher sees his task as that of describing an ideal
and considers it beneath his dignity to bother about operational
details, such as costs and inefficiencies. He is like an architect
who designs an aesthetically pleasing building and assumes that
engineers and accountants will figure out how to construct it and
pay for it.

One theme that has preoccupied intellectuals down through the years in their quest for a better world is income redistribution—that is, the idea of making everyone equal by taking from the rich and giving to the poor. In 400 B.C., Plato pointed to this goal in his great treatise *The Republic*. Sir Thomas More emphasized the point in his classic work *Utopia,* written in A.D. 1515. For centuries, Marxists and socialists have insisted that the principal job of government is to make society fairer by redistributing income.

It is remarkable that none of the philosophers and revolutionaries advocating income redistribution has ever stopped to ask whether the state is an efficient mechanism for accomplishing such a task. Intellectuals have argued late into the night over whether redistribution is moral or fair, but they have always assumed that the state would have no real problem carrying out this policy if it wanted to. Consider an analogy: an avant-garde intellectual proposes that airplanes be made of concrete but never considers the practical engineering aspect. He writes a lengthy, complex treatise, *The Justice of Concrete Airplanes.* Symposia are held on the subject; idealists and activists are inspired. "Yes, let's do it!" they say.

We would laugh at this spectacle because common sense tells us that concrete airplanes would not work very well. They probably would not fly at all! We realize that research needs to be done on matters of weight, lift, and thrust before we can take concrete airplanes seriously.

Well, when it comes to government spending programs, we do not have this kind of common sense. Practically no one realizes that research needs to be done on the efficiency of government transfers because the instinct to wonder about cost and waste is dulled by the illusion of the frictionless state. We suppose that government can shift wealth here and there without any significant overhead cost. Reformers do notice that, in practice, the policy of income redistribution seems to fail. They point with anger at the continuing gap between rich and poor in spite of a century of policies designed and enacted to shrink it, but they are unable to understand the failure of this policy because they do not inquire into overhead costs. It never occurs to them that redistribution programs might so distort incentives governing production and consumption that they can never significantly accomplish the aim of redistribution.

An inefficient policy of redistribution can, of course, be pressed harder and harder, as frustrated socialists around the world have done, seizing farms and factories and driving entrepreneurs into exile, unwittingly making war on prosperity. In the end, these idealists do indeed eliminate the gap between rich and poor—because everyone is made poor.

It's like saying a concrete airplane does fly . . . if you drop it off a bridge.

Indiana, Iowa, and Maine in Bondage

How much does the operation of the tax system cost? For anyone interested in the overhead cost of government programs, it's an important first question. Until we know the burden placed on society by the operation of the tax system, we cannot know whether any spending program is a wise idea because the benefit might be more than outweighed by the cost of raising the money to pay for it.

If I had been asked this question about the cost of the tax system in my student days, some fifty years ago, I would have answered, "Less than one percent of the taxes collected." That is what I had been told by teachers, by commentators, and by politicians. The reason why they and I so readily accepted this minuscule figure is that we all were swayed by the illusion of the frictionless state. We assumed that this godlike government could do its job neatly and efficiently. Furthermore, this number did seem to be verifiable: if you take the cost of the Internal Revenue Service and divide it into the total taxes flowing into the government, you come up with less than one percent.

For many years, I carried this number in my head, and, as a result, I believed that government spending programs represented excellent value for society. Then one day I received a CP-2000 letter in the mail from the IRS. This document accuses the tax-payer of not paying enough taxes and threatens collection action against him if he fails to give satisfaction. Having a gun pointed at my head spurred a high level of activity. I burrowed into my tax records, developed a theory to explain the IRS's blatantly wrong accusation, and drafted and redrafted a two-page, single-spaced letter. After months of anxiety, a form letter arrived saying there was no tax liability after all.

My feeling of relief was mingled with irritation. I had been forced to spend many precious hours using my talents as a writer and researcher to explain away a foolish clerical error. My time and effort—hundreds of dollars worth on a commercial basis—was wasted by the operation of the tax system. In this way, I began to realize that the overhead cost of the tax system is much higher than the on-budget cost of running the Internal Revenue Service. It involves wastes and costs that are imposed on citizens as they react to and attempt to comply with the tax system. My curiosity about these costs prompted me to undertake a book on the subject (*Costly Returns*, 1993).

I began by looking at tax-compliance costs—that is, the work done by businesses and individuals who have to study tax regulations, keep records, and fill out forms. The Arthur D. Little consulting firm had done a study of this burden in 1985; it came up with the figure of 5.4 *billion* man-hours. Updated to 1995, with more taxpayers and a more complex tax code, the number was 10.2 billion man-hours. This number translated to 5.5 million full-time workers—the equivalent of the entire workforce of Indiana, Iowa, and Maine combined—working all year long on just tax-compliance labors.

Then I compiled estimates for the different enforcement costs. I looked into the burden on citizens of having to participate in more than 1.5 million tax audits. I calculated the time wasted answering some 7 million written accusations like the one the IRS pestered me with—discovering, in the process, that the IRS knows that millions of these threatening accusations are erroneous. In a typical year, some 18 million Americans are the object of some tax-enforcement action.

The tax system's most important overhead burden is the disincentive cost. In economic terms, a tax is the same as a fine: it is a penalty for engaging in certain behavior. We all understand that a fine discourages the relevant activity: a fine against speeding discourages speeding, a fine against littering discourages littering, and so on. Both lawmakers and the public strangely forget that the same principle applies to taxes. If you tax income, you are essentially levying a fine on constructive activities that produce income—working, opening new businesses, increasing production. Hence, you will have less work, less investment, and less production.

To illustrate the point, imagine that the government taxes 100 percent of income. You go to the factory, work all day, and come home with . . . nothing. No one would go to work under these conditions. The government would have achieved total economic ruin with its tax system. A 50 percent income tax would not be so ruinous, but it would still depress economic activity, leaving the country poorer than it otherwise would be, leaving workers unemployed, factories not producing, and so on.

How large is the disincentive effect of the existing U.S. tax system? This question is complicated because many different taxes and tax rates are involved. In recent years, economists have begun to estimate these costs and have come up with figures ranging from 24 to 151 percent of total taxes collected. After reviewing this literature for my book, I concluded that the best overall estimate was given by a study in the 1985 *American Economic Review* that advanced the figure of 33.2 percent. When I added this number to all the other tax system overhead costs—compliance, enforcement, litigation, and so on—the total came to 65.01 percent. In other words, in order to bring $100 in taxes into the Treasury, government imposes additional costs and wastes on the public amounting to $65. This 65 percent figure was more than one hundred times the on-budget cost of running the IRS (which was 0.61 percent). Instead of being a virtually frictionless machine for extracting wealth from the American people, the tax system turns out to be appallingly destructive.

A Frustrated Firefighter

Unfortunately, the bad news doesn't end there. Once the government has the money it has forced from the people, it has to have systems for giving it out, of directing it to the purposes intended. These systems of spending money also entail costs and wastes, which together can be called the "overhead cost of disbursement."

To begin with, there are *administrative costs*—that is, the expense of running the bureaucracy that gives the money away. You can't just dump the money in a pile in the street for people to take as they wish. You have to create rules and regulations that specify who gets how much, and it takes a bureaucracy to apply these regulations. For example, in the federal food stamp program (nicely called the Supplemental Nutrition Assistance Program), the cost of operating the federal and state agencies that administer the program amounts to 16 percent of total spending on the program.

Next there are *misallocation costs,* which refers to bureaucracy's misuse of labor and capital. Government agencies are shielded from the discipline of the market. Being based on the coercion of the tax system, they do not have to be efficient to please consumers: the tax dollars will keep flowing in almost regardless of how ineffective, wasteful, or corrupt they become. Furthermore, government agencies have many political masters, which means government employees are hemmed in by many burdensome and conflicting regulations. They are discouraged from exercising initiative, from acting independently, from taking risks. In the end, these bureaucratic restraints lead to a lack of enthusiasm, a "why bother?" attitude that impairs organization efficiency.

My introduction to government's misallocation problem came in my student days when I worked with a surveying crew in Idaho for the U.S. Forest Service. In my first week on the job, four of us were called out on a Sunday afternoon to deal with a fire around a tree that had been struck by lightning. When we drove up, flames were leaping high around the tree. As a city kid from New Jersey given an opportunity to save a forest, I was excited and eager to be the hero. I rushed in with my sprayer can and started squirting water on the flames.

"Payne!" yelled the crew boss. "Cut that out! Come over here and sit down!"

I did as I was told and joined the others, who were resting and smoking in the shade. At first, I couldn't understand why we were not fighting the fire. Then I glanced over at the tree, and I began to understand. The flames were lower than before. The fire was going out on its own! The crew boss was trying to make the fire last as long as possible so we could earn more overtime. We could have put it out in fifteen minutes and gone home; instead, the crew boss helped us all get many hours of overtime. After all, it was no skin off his nose: he was spending government money.

This kind of routine inefficiency means that it costs more to do anything with a government agency than with a normal private firm. In 1981, George Mason University economists James T. Bennett and Manuel H. Johnson reviewed the cost of publicly provided services and compared them with private providers in the fields of trash collection, fire protection, ship repair, airlines, and ambulance service. Their research led them to promulgate the "Bureaucratic Rule of Two": on average, it costs government twice as much as a market-based provider to deliver the same service. The misallocation cost, in other words, amounts to a 50 percent waste factor. Studies in other fields show the same pattern. Public schools, for example, cost twice as much per pupil as private schools.

The waste that goes on in government agencies is only part of the disbursement cost. The other component is the waste in the private sector that occurs in connection with the subsidy. To start with, there is the *subsidy compliance cost*. You have to apply for most subsidies, which uses up time and resources. Getting food stamps, for example, requires visiting the appropriate offices, waiting in line, and supplying some sixty pieces of required information. Recipients may think food stamps are "free," but they actually have to *work* for them. A few days ago I was chatting with a North Dakota farmer about the farm subsidies he received. He was complaining mightily about the complex and confusing paperwork they involved. I asked him how much of his working day he spent on this paperwork. He thought a moment. "Fifteen to 20 percent" was his reply.

Applying for government grants—in science, education, environment—can be very costly, involving professional grant writers and other specialists. These grant applications can involve thousands of pages and cartons of supporting documents. In the arts, where government agencies often dole out funds in small amounts, sometimes just a few thousand dollars, grant-preparation costs may equal or exceed the amount of the grant! Another component of the compliance burden is the reporting cost. After the money is given, agencies demand that the recipient answer questionnaires and file reports and financial documents, all of which takes time and effort.

Another burden of subsidies comes from the way they can encourage recipients to leave economic resources idle. A simple example is paying farmers not to produce crops. The cost of this subsidy is not just the payments to the farmers but, in addition, the production the country loses by keeping the farmer's land, labor, and equipment idle. We can call this type of waste the *lost-production cost.*

The magnitude of this cost varies depending on the nature of the subsidy. High lost-production costs are found in programs that encourage people not to work. Disability payments are an example. The Social Security Administration spends more than $100 billion a year to support 13 million people who claim a physical or mental disability. To obtain this benefit, the recipients hire lawyers and attend hearings to prove they cannot work (a subsidy compliance cost that runs into many thousands of dollars in each case). Once obtained, the subsidy would be lost if the claimant proves himself not disabled by, for example, *working*. In this way, the Social Security Administration encourages millions of people not to work—people who are less disabled than many people not on the program who are working and contributing to society. This program's lost production cost runs into billions of lost working hours.

This is not to say disability subsidies are right or wrong. They may be needed and helpful in certain cases. I take no position on this question. The point here is simply that the true cost of such a program is more than its on-budget expenditure. It includes the value of the labor that would have been contributed to the nation's wealth in the absence of the program.

Yet another disbursement burden is the *overconsumption cost.* Whenever government supplies a good or service for free or at below cost, people will consume more of it than they would if they were paying for it out of their own pocket. This excess consumption is, in economic terms, waste. For example, a woman of my acquaintance was given thirty pounds of butter by a Department of Agriculture commodities program. She found the butter was taking up too much space in her freezer, so she threw most of it in the trash. She gave five pounds of it to me, which I tried to use, but in the end I also had to throw most of it away.

A few years ago a friend and I had hip-replacement operations. His, paid for by Medicare, cost $45,000; mine, paid for out of my own pocket, cost $15,000. Overconsumption mainly accounted for the difference. My doctor—who knew I was paying my own way—helped me get out of the hospital early, in just two days. My friend, with "free" hospital care, stayed four days. I recuperated at home; my friend took advantage of six weeks in a nursing home. I did rehabilitation work on my own; my friend was happy to let his "free" program pay a physical therapist $75 an hour to watch him ride an exercise bike. (There was also a significant administrative cost difference: my providers gave me a 20 percent discount for cash because they didn't have to wrestle with the paperwork of reimbursement.)

The True Cost of Cross-Subsidy

In table 1, I have listed fourteen of the principal overhead costs in government transfer programs. In a rationally-managed government, one would expect to see many similar outlines, or much more extensive ones, in Treasury offices, budget departments, and congressional finance committees. And you would expect to find hundreds of calculations of the overhead costs involved in different government programs. After all, until you have assessed the overhead costs of programs, it is impossible to know whether they do more good than harm.

Now, here is the surprise: you will not find any such table anywhere in government, and you will not find a single calculation—not even an approximate estimate—of the full overhead cost of any government program! Policymakers roundly ignore the overhead cost issue. What they see—assuming they have managed to overcome the philanthropic illusion—is that money is taken from one group of people and shifted to another. Then, in other subsidy programs, money is shifted back. This system of cross-subsidy may not do as much good as people think, they're willing to admit, but what's the harm in it?

Table 1. Overhead Costs of Government Transfers

Costs of Taxation

1. Governmental administrative cost

Private-sector costs:

2. Compliance cost
3. Dealing with audits and accusations
4. Tax litigation cost
5. Dealing with forced collections
6. Economic disincentive cost
7. Disincentive cost of tax uncertainty
8. Evasion and avoidance costs

Costs of Disbursement

9. Governmental administrative cost
10. Governmental misallocation cost

Private-sector costs:

11. Consumer overconsumption cost
12. Consumer application cost
13. Consumer reporting cost
14. Lost production cost

Some years ago I asked a senior staff member of the U.S. Senate Budget Committee whether she was worried about the problem of cross-subsidy. She wasn't. "It evens out," she said. "Everybody pays for everyone else's goods." She assumed she was being frank and hard-boiled in putting it this way, but in truth she revealed an astonishing naïveté.

The idea that this system of cross-subsidy "evens out" would be true only if there were no significant overhead costs in the state's system of transferring resources. If one recognizes these costs, then it is immediately apparent that in a system where "everyone pays for everyone else's goods," *everyone* loses—big time! Consider the case where the average person pays the average amount of tax and receives an average level of benefit. The overhead cost of taxation is 65 percent; that is, to get $100 to spend on something, government puts an additional burden of $65 on the average person, so the total burden is $165. Then disbursement costs (misallocation, overconsumption, etc.) eat up a high proportion of the $100 being spent. For this illustration, let's make the conservative assumption that disbursement costs amount to half of the appropriated funds (employing the Bureaucratic Rule of Two noted earlier). This means that the average person ends up contributing a total of $165 in order to get $50 worth of a government benefit. The cross-subsidy system is not a harmless transfer system that "evens out." It is an erosion of wealth that makes everyone much poorer than they would otherwise be.

Citizen ignorance of overhead costs accounts for much of the popular appeal of subsidies. Consider Medicare, widely regarded as a successful or at least desirable government program. If the transfer system were frictionless, the program might be defensible: the average person over his lifetime would get approximately the same dollars in medical benefits that he paid in taxes. Unfortunately, this is not what is happening. The overhead costs of taxation and the overhead costs of disbursement should also be taken into consideration. The result is that the average person pays many times what the medical care is worth. The hip operation that would have cost someone $15,000 if paid for out of his own pocket ends up costing him $45,000 when the money is cycled through government's tax-and-spend system.

I'm sure those who are fond of government would wish to question my suggestion that government tax-and-spend programs involve such a staggering waste. My response is, please do! By all means, look for other estimates of the overhead costs of government transfer programs. If you do look, however, you will encounter, as I noted above, a surprising void. No one seems to be interested in compiling this statistic. Medical care is an example. Despite the fact that thousands of administrators and academics analyze the economics of government health care programs, none of these experts has come forth with an estimate of these programs' full overhead cost.

One sign of the shallowness in this field is the way in which analysts and debaters focus on administrative costs. Backers of an expanded government role point out that the administrative costs in government's Medicare program are only 3 percent of spending, whereas the administrative costs of (government subsidized) private health insurance are 13 percent of spending. The point, even if the numbers are sound, is unimportant. As table 1 shows, there are at least *fourteen* overhead costs in a government transfer system. Many of these costs—such as the tax compliance costs, the tax disincentive cost, the misallocation cost, and the overconsumption cost—are vastly larger than the administrative cost. The overconsumption cost alone is probably at least 100 percent of spending. Those who debate health care costs in terms of the miniscule administrative expense are revealing an appalling lack of awareness of the whole picture.

What accounts for the lack of interest in overhead costs? Cynics will say that politicians and administrators ignore the subject because they are irresponsible demagogues, happy to approve programs that make them look good, and who don't care about the waste and harm in these programs. I believe that assessment is too harsh. The lawmakers, administrators, and health care policy experts who are ignoring the overhead costs of health care subsidies are for the most part sincere and well intentioned. They believe they are operating basically helpful programs.

I believe the reason why they make no serious effort to analyze overhead costs is that they don't imagine that these costs can be so staggeringly high. They don't imagine that their governmental systems of providing medical care might be forcing John Doe to pay *five times as much* for the *same* medical care he would have obtained in a private, pay-as-you-go system. They don't imagine this kind of waste because they have fallen victim to the illusion of the frictionless state. They believe—along with the general public and generations of social philosophers—that government can transfer resources without any significant overhead cost.

This is not to say that a government subsidy program such as health care is necessarily wrong. Maybe a system with a 400 percent waste factor has virtues that outweigh this cost. My point is simply that it is irrational to discuss such subsidies without considering this waste. If a child says, "I think a concrete airplane would be neat," we are right to laugh because we can see that he has no idea what he is talking about. If he says, "I think a concrete airplane would fly because the lift of eight pounds per square foot of wing surface will overcome the weight of seventeen tons," we do not laugh. We may question his figures, but we can see he has at least begun to grasp the underlying relationships.

Similarly, if a politician says, "I am for government's provision of affordable health care for all Americans," we should be skeptical because he is assuming no significant waste in the subsidy he proposes. If he says, "I am for government's provision of affordable health care for all Americans, and the waste factor in my program will be only 238 percent," we may begin to take him seriously. We may disagree with the number, but we can see that he has at least overcome the illusion that government can supply benefits with no significant overhead cost.

4

The Materialistic Illusion

Why the War on Poverty Failed

In 1964, President Lyndon Johnson declared "an unconditional war on poverty in America," proposing an array of new programs to help the poor. "We shall not rest until that war is won," he said. "The richest nation on earth can afford to win it."

As the decades passed, it became increasingly clear that the war on poverty had failed. It certainly had failed to "cure" poverty, as Johnson promised, and many observers wondered if the federal largesse had not made the problem worse. One of those skeptical observers was Michael Janofsky, a reporter for the *New York Times*. In February 1998, he wrote a front-page story on poverty in rural Kentucky, detailing the failure of the war on poverty in the one region that was supposed to be the centerpiece of reform. "Federal and state agencies have plowed billions of dollars into Appalachia," he wrote, yet the area "looks much as it did 30 years ago, when President Lyndon B. Johnson declared a war on poverty, taking special aim at the rural decay."

Janofsky visited Owsley County, Kentucky, and found a poverty rate of 46 percent, with more than half the adults illiterate and half of them unemployed. "Feelings of hopelessness have become so deeply entrenched," he reported, "that many residents have long forsaken any expectation of bettering themselves." For years, the government had been trying to treat the despair with welfare programs: two-thirds of the inhabitants were receiving federal assistance, including food stamps, Assistance to Families with Dependent Children payments, and Supplemental Security Income (SSI) disability payments. This assistance, it appeared, was part of the area's problems.

"The war on poverty was the worst thing that ever happened to Appalachia," Janofsky quoted one resident as saying. "It gave people a way to get by without having to do any work." Local officials told him that "many parents urge their children to try to go to special education classes at school as a way to prove they are eligible for SSI disability benefits." (The senior class at the local high school picked as its motto, "I came, I slept, I graduated.")

Why did the war on poverty fail? The government had spent more than $5 trillion attempting to solve the problems of the poor, yet came up empty. Perhaps the best way to explain the debacle is to take a close look at the book that inspired the war on poverty, Michael Harrington's *The Other America*, published in 1962. The most influential policy book of the day, *The Other America* was cited again and again by the politicians, activists, and administrators who set up welfare programs in the 1960s. In it, we find the fallacy that sent reformers down dark and tangled paths into today's social tragedies.

Harrington's premise was that poverty is a purely economic problem: the needy simply lack the material resources to lead productive, happy lives. Supply these resources, the theory runs, and you will have solved the problem of poverty. "The means are at hand," declared Harrington, "to fulfill the age-old dream: poverty can now be abolished." Another book from that era boldly challenged biblical wisdom with its title: *The Poor Ye Need Not Have with You*. This 1970 volume was written by Robert Levine, who had served in the Office of Economic Opportunity, the federal government's antipoverty agency. His book was supported by the Ford Foundation and the Urban Institute, two principal backers of the war on poverty. For Levine, curing poverty was a simple matter of algebra: "Even a quick look can convince us that poverty as it is currently defined in the United States is a completely solvable problem," he wrote. "If we were to provide every last poor family and individual in the United States with enough income to bring them above the level of poverty, the required outlay would be less than $10 billion a year."

The assumption behind such confident declarations is *the materialistic illusion: the belief that money alone buys public-policy results*. Both Levine and Harrington assumed that the only thing needed to cure poverty is the application of physical resources toward that end.

The materialistic illusion originates in a half-truth: physical resources are indeed essential to fulfill any objective or to carry on any activity. To climb a mountain, you need boots, ropes, and pitons. Those who say that the best things in life are free haven't thought about the physical inputs that keep them alive, such as food and shelter, and other resources that make experiences possible. The sunset at the beach may be free, but the car to drive there costs money.

Although physical inputs may be important for success, however, these inputs alone are not sufficient. The human beings receiving the money must have the skill and motivation to put that money to constructive use. Let's put this idea in a simple formula:

$$\text{Outcome} = (M)(H),$$

where M is money or material resources, H represents the human variables of motivation and ability, and the outcome is the product of the two variables.

To illustrate this formula, suppose we want brain surgery performed. In order for that to happen, there must be some material inputs: the instruments, the lights, the hospital room. And for it to happen on a regular, long-term basis, the surgeon has to eat. So if M is zero, no surgery can take place. But there are human factors, too. If we offered someone on the street $1 million to do brain surgery, we would not have a successful result because this passerby would not have the skill. H in this case would be zero. If we paid him $2 million, we would still get a zero result: $2 million times zero is zero.

When we grapple with problems in our daily lives, we are well aware of the human factors needed to make the expenditure of money useful. We don't buy our nine-year-old son a car, and we don't give money to our shiftless cousin. When our attention turns to public policy, however, we are less aware of the human factors. National problems are treated as large, abstract blocks: "unemployment," "substance abuse," "illiteracy." The individuals involved in these broad problems are lost from view—and so are their values and motivation. Money, in contrast, is a simple concept, easy to grasp, so it looms large in our thinking. In effect, on public-policy questions we interpret the formula to look like this:

$$\text{Outcome} = (M)_{(H)}$$

We end up virtually ignoring the human factors and succumb to the materialistic illusion, the belief that money alone solves public problems.

This was the error that the poverty warriors made. They assumed that by giving money to poor people, they could improve their lives. They were so far away from the individuals they were trying to help that they didn't notice the importance of the human factors in the policy outcome.

Making the Problem Worse

Many of those who went along with the war on poverty did not embrace all the rhetoric about these programs. They knew that poverty was a complex problem, one not easily solved in a stroke. They endorsed the effort, however, thinking that at least the programs were better than doing nothing. It's the attitude that a passerby has when he gives a beggar a dollar. He knows the dollar won't turn the beggar's life around, but, he reasons, it is a step in the right direction. Unfortunately, the idea that spending always represents a degree of help is often an unsound assumption.

A close look at the formula just given illustrates where this thinking can go wrong. If the human factor, H, is small but positive, then, yes, adding more money will produce a small but positive outcome. But consider the possibility that H is negative. Our high school algebra tells us that a minus times a plus is a minus.

Hence, the formula says that in the case where H is negative, the more money you pour into a situation, the worse the outcome!

I can illustrate the point with the example of the beggar. If the beggar uses the donated dollar to buy healthy food—an example of a positive use of the money—then the donation does him some good. But if he uses it to buy alcohol, so that he gets drunk, he ends up worse off. If the donor gave the beggar still more money and the beggar spent it in the same destructive way, this bigger contribution sends him into a bigger, more destructive binge.

This paradox—that programs to help the poor can actually end up harming them—was perhaps first formally noted by the Commission on Poor Law Reform in England in 1832. The charity experts examining the British systems of giving food and clothing on a regular basis found this support was having an *incapacitation effect,* luring some people into staying poor instead of exerting themselves to rise to better situations. An unemployment benefit, for example, may enable the recipient to move to another city and get a job. But that assumes the recipient is motivated to make the effort. If the recipient is unmotivated, he will take the money to live on and simply remain unemployed. In effect, the benefit lures the poorly motivated recipient into a dysfunctional—and suffering—lifestyle.

In the English town of Exmouth, where I lived in 1993, I encountered a victim of the incapacitation effect. He was a middle-aged man who spent many hours of the day leaning on the railing of a bridge over a disused railway line. His routine puzzled me, and one day I stopped to talk to him. He had been a fireman on this branch railway line, which had closed some twenty-five years earlier. He had begun work when he was eighteen and was laid off at age twenty-six when the line was shut down. "I gave the best years of my life to that railway," he said bitterly. The statement rather shocked me because I was about his age—early fifties—and I assumed that some of the best years of my life still lay ahead.

This embittered former railwayman had been unemployed since his job gave out. I don't know what combination of assistance he relied on—whether a lifetime severance bonus from the railway or other welfare payments. Whatever it was, it enabled him to get by without working.

"I gave the best years of my life to that railway," he kept repeating during our conversation. It seemed a line from a labor union agitator's stump speech, but this man had made it the focus of his life. When originally preached, the slogan was no doubt used to defend hefty payments to laid-off workers—which may have seemed fair and helpful at the time. But look at the long-run result. Though cushioned from want, this man was far from happy. He didn't die at age twenty-six. Two decades later he was still a healthy human being, capable of productively occupying himself, capable of proudly making a gainful living. The unemployment payments had helped draw him into a state of permanent idleness, wasting his life sullenly gazing down the grassy trench of an empty railway line.

The incapacitation effect helps explain why the war on poverty missed the mark so badly. As *Times* reporter Janofsky found in rural Kentucky, if the human factors are negative, then spending money to help the poor does not buy happiness, but rather unhappiness.

A Culture of Discontent

Great Britain has a long tradition of philosophers and activists who dramatized the plight of the poor and urged government programs to alleviate their suffering. Give those at the bottom money and free services, they argued, and social vices will fade away. The father will no longer have to steal bread to feed his children; the mother would not have to escape her harsh world by resorting to gin. The reformers' theories and political activism culminated in one of the most extensive welfare states in the world, a society where government provides a vast range of payments and free services to the poor. According to the reformers, these benefits should have transformed the poorest of the poor into virtuous participants in the life of the nation. The reality, for those at the bottom of the economic scale in Britain, has turned out quite differently.

Frank Field is a long-time British Labour member of Parliament who has served in many high government posts, including the Privy Council and the Cabinet. For the first decades of his political career, he was one of the reformers, penning dozens of books and pamphlets urging more government spending to alleviate the plight of the poor. Then in the 1990s he began to notice a worrisome trend: members of the lower classes had not been turned into contented and productive citizens. Instead, they were malcontents who were terrorizing his decent, law-abiding constituents. The strange thing about their harassment of decent folk was that they were not engaging in crime for personal gain, but expressing a viciousness whose aim was merely to cause distress to others: "Young lads . . . ran across [neighbors'] bungalow roofs, peed through their letterboxes, jumped out of the shadows as they returned home at night, and, when they were watching television, tried to break their sitting room windows, presumably with the hope of showering the pensioners with shattered glass."

The local ambulance service in Field's hometown was undermined by hostile behavior: thugs threw bricks and slates at the vehicles and looted unattended ambulances. Some lower-class families—regularly in need of ambulance service because of crises involving drugs, alcohol, and fighting—were so hostile that ambulance crews needed police protection when they came to serve them.

Field found this pattern of corrosive incivility so alarming that he wrote a book about it, *Neighbours from Hell* (2003). The breakdown in civility, he argues, reverses a long historical evolution where families learned to transmit social virtues and common decencies. "These virtues, which became almost universally practiced, ensured that the family's behaviour promoted a thoughtfulness for its other members as well as its neighbors." He is at a loss to explain the cause of what he calls a "new barbarism," though he is painfully aware that this barbarism contradicts the reformers' dreams: "The center-left's belief was that an amelioration of the grosser forms of inequality would speed the march of civilization. Merely to recite the phrase throws into sharp relief how these idealist hopes have been dashed."

For an explanation of this troubling trend toward lower-class disrespect, we can turn to another British writer, Theodore Dalrymple (a pen name). Dalrymple is a psychiatrist who works in a prison hospital and in a hospital in a poor neighborhood of an English city. This vantage point enables him to observe large numbers of poor people in painful circumstances and to explore the patterns of thought and behavior that have led to their suffering. He reports his conclusions in his book on the British underclass, *Life at the Bottom* (2001).

The strange feature of twenty-first-century Britain, Dalrymple finds, is how little the suffering of the poor has to do with material poverty. Instead, distress seems to be self-inflicted, caused by individuals' flaunting of commonsense principles of success-ful living. For example, many of Dalrymple's patients have tat-tooed themselves heavily, often with objectionable phrases such as "FUCK OFF" placed quite visibly on their anatomy. These der-matological expressions of discontent not only cost them money to obtain in the first place, but also impede their ability to get a job or make other constructive contacts to better their lives. In their social behavior, members of the underclass live out their bel-ligerent tattoos. They are sullen, rude, and deliberately unhelpful. They do not merely let trash fall on the street; they fling it down in anger.

Dalrymple traces this lack of consideration to the material benefits given out by the British welfare state. He uses the hous-ing market as an example. In a natural housing market, landlords want tenants with good values who will take care of their property. Hence, "selfish" landlords reinforce healthy social values: honesty, courtesy, decorum, stable family life. Government housing agen-cies, in contrast, give housing to those who seem to need it the most, and in this way they can reward antisocial behavior.

This perverse value system has become internalized in the thinking of members of the underclass. When patients seeking public housing ask Dalrymple to write letters of recommenda-tion, he reports, they want him to highlight their dysfunctional behavior—their drug addiction or gambling problems. "In not a single case," he writes, "has anyone ever asked me to write that he is a decent, hardworking citizen who would make a good tenant. That would send him straight to the bottom of the waiting list."

In other words, it appears that a pattern of perverse social learning takes place in response to the welfare benefits. Centu-ries ago, when life was hard and resources scarce, it paid to be courteous and cooperative: your life depended on it. You learned to behave considerately toward neighbors who might give you a job, a cloak, or a crust of bread. Parents taught their children that being eager to serve others was the way to get ahead. Children who weren't taught—or who didn't learn—this lesson did not survive. The result was that, over the centuries, habits of civility developed. When the welfare state came along, however, supplying every material need, it no longer became necessary to cultivate neighbors' good will.

This theory may explain why members of the underclass don't need to be civil toward neighbors, but it doesn't explain why they are so pointedly angry and self-destructive. Dalrymple traces this hostility to the psychological depression that overtakes lives that are "empty of purpose." Providing one's own food and shelter is one of the great steadying and invigorating life motives, especially for younger, less sophisticated individuals. In the welfare state, mere survival is no achievement, though, because the state provides everything. Thus, the welfare state denies its beneficiaries the self-respect that comes from feeding and housing oneself and one's family.

Dalrymple points out that this loss of self-respect makes the British poor especially unfortunate when compared to the poor in third-world countries, such as in Tanzania and Nigeria, for example, where he has worked: "Nothing I saw—neither the poverty nor the overt oppression—ever had the same devastating effect on the human personality as the undiscriminating welfare state. I never saw the loss of dignity, the spiritual and emotional vacuity, or the sheer ignorance of how to live that I see daily in England. . . . The worst poverty is in England—and it is not a material poverty but poverty of soul."

The irony of the modern welfare state, which allows its subjects such wonderful freedom to behave however they like, is that it develops a subculture of *unhappiness*. The pointless rudeness, the sullen demeanor, the lack of interest in the outside world, the lack of ambition: all are signs of serious depression. In the British underclass, this "willful chasing after misery," as Dalrymple puts it, shows up in a number of unfortunate social trends. First, there is the high and rising rate of crime and vandalism. Second, Britain has one of the highest rates of attempted suicide in the world. More than 120,000 people a year go through painful episodes of half-trying to take their own lives. These attempts are, of course, unconscious cries for help, yet the authorities only know how to treat the victims by redoubling the application of material goods and services.

It is right to be concerned about the plight of the poor. Our humanity and our compassion demand that we seek ways to lift up those who suffer. How to make this charitable impulse effective is a complicated problem that raises many questions. Perhaps government programs need to be greatly restructured, or perhaps government programs should be abandoned in favor of local, personal methods of assistance. This is not the place to debate these questions. My point is simply that in these matters one needs to transcend the naive assumption that if you appropriate money to help the poor, you necessarily help the poor.

Throwing Money at Problems

The materialistic illusion applies not just to government's efforts to help the poor, but to everything that it might try to accomplish. Unsophisticated observers assume government money can provide any useful service a society might need. They see government as a store with social goods for sale: green energy, education, art, housing, job training, and so forth. If you want more, you simply buy more.

The error in this thinking is that it overlooks the human factor again. In order for an agency to deliver job training, let us say, it does need physical resources; it has to pay for wages, telephones, photocopiers, and so on. But if the human factors aren't right, these physical inputs will be unavailing. Our formula applies:

$$\text{Outcome} = (M)(H),$$

where M is the money appropriated, and H refers to the human factors—the motivation and abilities of people in the agency. If the human variables are deficient, pouring all the money in the world into the agency may produce no achievement at all. And if H is negative, as it would be if employees had improper motives or wrongheaded theories, then the outcome can be negative: the program will do more harm than good. The public often overlooks this possibility because it tends to assume that the people staffing every government agency know how to accomplish the assigned goals and that they are motivated to do so. This assumption is often unrealistic.

The field of job training illustrates the problem. Researchers who have looked closely at these programs are often surprised at how much money is being spent without actually moving clients into the workforce. In 2006, *Washington Post* reporter Neil Irwin looked into job-training programs in the District of Columbia and discovered that despite the sixty-one government programs administered by twenty-four different federal and local agencies, unemployment, especially among the unskilled workers whom job training is supposed to help, remained high. It was puzzling—scandalous, actually—that these many programs were not moving workers into jobs, especially considering that employers at the time were eager for workers.

One explanation for such failure is that most job-training agencies inadvertently inculcate bad work habits. The problem is that the programs are funded according to the number of students enrolled. If students are criticized or disciplined for being late, lazy, or rude, they tend to drop out, lowering class numbers and therefore lowering the payments to the providers. Hence, teachers ignore uncooperative behavior.

Reporter Ken Auletta discovered this perverse effect when he looked into a job-training program in New York City in the early 1980s. The program, run by the federally funded Manpower Development Research Corporation, claimed in its brochure that it aimed to instill "positive work habits and attitudes." To implement this goal, it announced certain standards, including firm rules requiring on-time attendance. When Auletta attended one of the classes, however, he discovered that the rules were not being applied. Students were allowed to come and go as they wished, even to sleep or read newspapers in class. When Auletta asked about the theory of instilling work discipline, the trainer in charge explained that if the rules were applied, "we'd lose just about everyone in the class." The result, as Auletta reported in his book *The Underclass* (1983), a program that was supposed "to induce trainees to accept responsibility for their own fate" actually reinforced irresponsibility and made the clients *less* prepared to enter the workforce than before they took the "training."

Swayed by the materialistic illusion, lawmakers ignore this kind of problem in service delivery. They assume that money necessarily buys the desired policy result. They believe that if you want more job training, you should spend more money on job training. One sign of this materialistic mentality is the way debaters evaluate policy success according to the amount of money spent. For example, in criticizing the Ronald Reagan administration for its insensitivity to the plight of the poor, *Time* magazine asserted in October 1988 that "subsidized housing has been slashed 77 percent." Reagan's housing secretary was happy to debate on these materialistic terms. "Wrong," he replied. Spending, he claimed, "has been doubled." Neither side stopped to question the idea of equating money spent with a policy result.

Scientific research is another field where money inputs are assumed to guarantee policy results. Lawmakers want solutions to social, economic, and technological problems, but they don't stop to notice that successful scientific research depends on many intangible human factors. The scientists involved in the research might be pursuing a misguided theory; they might be mired in tradition; they might lack imagination or originality; they might waste their energy in petty quarrels; they might be lazy. Given the importance of such human factors, doubling the funds spent on cancer research, let us say, may well mean no increase whatsoever in useful research findings. It may merely result in carpets twice as thick in scientists' offices.

The corrective for the materialistic illusion is to recognize explicitly that nonmonetary factors bear on policy results. Such recognition may not be easy in the superficial context of self-promotion and point scoring in political life. Politicians, administrators, and pressure groups have a strong interest in presenting policy results as simple goods, such as wheat or steel, which can be purchased with a snap of the fingers. This impulse should be countered by avoiding language that equates spending with a policy outcome. Instead of saying, "We should spend more money on education," one should recognize the uncertainty involved by saying something like, "We should spend more money *intended for education*," or "We should spend more money *in the hope that it will improve education*."

Readers will say that it is unrealistic to expect politicians to be so thoughtful, and to give up the propaganda value of trading on the materialistic illusion. Perhaps so. My goal here is not to abolish the distortions of politics, but merely to help thoughtful reformers stay clear of them.

5

The Watchful Eye Illusion

Government as God

In 2008, the United States suffered a financial shock that left investors gasping for air. The bubble in real estate prices burst, leaving millions of property owners with negative equity, owing more on their properties than they were worth. Many credit institutions had made "subprime" loans, which essentially were loans to buyers who couldn't afford to repay them. When these buyers defaulted, the lending institutions took huge losses. Large brokerage houses, including Bear Sterns and Merrill Lynch, had so mismanaged their investments that they ended up deeply in debt. Insurance giant AIG faced the same problem of unsound investments and insolvency.

Facing this worrisome financial scene, incoming president Barack Obama promised in his inaugural address on January 20, 2009, to use government to prevent future mishaps. The market has good aspects, he said. "Its power to generate wealth and expand freedom is unmatched, but this crisis has reminded us that without a watchful eye, the market can spin out of control."

At first glance, this view seems plausible. No one can deny that some of the people involved in market activities—investors, brokers, bankers—are inept, short-sighted, or dishonest. Because of their human failings, harmful outcomes are possible. For example, thoughtless investors, responding more to emotion than reasoned analysis, can feed a speculative bubble. They get carried away by the idea that some industry or product is the wave of the future. When the bubble pops, the contraction in economic activity is felt on Main Street. Or, to mention another possibility, a dishonest salesman might peddle shares in a bogus company, leaving investors with losses when the fraud is discovered. To prevent such unfortunate episodes, many say, the market should be supervised and regulated by the watchful eye of government.

Few pause to examine the underlying rationale of this seemingly plausible advice: it assumes that government officials are immune to the failings and weaknesses of people outside government. This assumption might be plausible if these officials came from a distinct social caste with an extraordinary genetic endowment. If they were raised from birth by strict nannies and taught exceptional academic and moral standards in special schools, they might be better than the rest of us. But government officials do not have distinctive genes, background, or education. The businessman we mistrusted because of his shady dealings in real estate can become a senator. The banker who was shortsighted in managing investments becomes an undersecretary of the Treasury. Holding the different post doesn't make him wiser or more responsible.

The idea that government has superior wisdom is to some extent rooted in the tendency to view government as godlike, an impulse that goes back many millennia. In ancient times, rulers were thought to be divine. As this view broke down, it was replaced by the idea that rulers were agents of God, and there-fore anyone who questioned their decisions was questioning God. To some degree, this veneration of government has faded, but the need to worship authority has not entirely disappeared. The world is a confusing, challenging place, posing problems that humans often cannot understand. They find it reassuring to believe in some higher, wiser entity that can keep them from harm. In effect, in modern times, government has become the god in which we no longer believe. When financial markets are crashing about our ears, we look to this superior being, who, from his Olympian position, surveys the scene and controls error and wrongdoing.

This is the *watchful eye illusion: the idea that government has greater knowledge and wisdom than the public.* It is a fallacy because government officials are made of the same human stuff as the rest of us. A look at the market failures Obama alluded to in his speech bears this out. Take the speculative bubble in housing. Did senators see the danger before the rest of us and pass laws to limit the purchase of real estate? Of course not: they participated in the housing boom along with everyone else.

Another example is the subprime lending boom that col-lapsed in 2008. Legislators did not forbid banks to lend to homebuyers with poor credit. To the contrary: it was the poli-ticians who passed the Community Reinvestment Act in 1977, legislation that, as implemented, all but forced banks to lend to borrowers with poor credit ratings. Did these lawmakers forbid the government housing agencies Fannie Mae and Freddie Mac from buying the subprime loans? No, they encouraged and pro-tected these institutions, even as analysts warned they were dan-gerously overextended.

It is not even clear that government officials can catch fraudulent securities dealers before they do harm. After all, those who engage in deceptive practices look like respectable managers and trustworthy investment advisors. That's why they fool ordinary investors. It is unreasonable to expect government officials to be alert and energetic Lone Rangers, seeking out fires where no one else even sees smoke.

Even when bureaucrats are given smoke to smell, they may be reluctant to suspect fire. The case of Bernie Madoff, who took in a reported $65 billion in a fraudulent "Ponzi" investment scheme, illustrates the point. A few insiders in the investment world knew something was fishy about his company. One, Harry Markopolos, spotted the fraud in 1999 and sent the U.S. Securities and Exchange Commission (SEC) a detailed report listing twenty-nine reasons why, as he entitled his report, "the world's largest hedge fund is a fraud." The SEC looked into the matter and found nothing wrong. After the scandal broke in 2008, the embarrassed chairman of the SEC, Christopher Cox, bemoaned his staff's "multiple failures" that caused them to miss the fraud.

The history of the Office of Thrift Supervision (OTS) gives an interesting lesson in government's abilities to know about and control financial irresponsibility. This agency was created in 1989 in reaction to the collapse of many savings-and-loan institutions that had overextended themselves taking advantage of government deposit insurance. In signing the legislation creating the OTS, President George H. W. Bush said, "It will safeguard and stabilize America's financial system and put in place permanent reforms so these problems will never happen again."

Time, as Machiavelli said, is the father of truth. Twenty years after the savings-and-loan scandal, the OTS proved to be entirely ineffective as a high-level financial regulator: it did nothing to prevent the financial collapses of 2008. When it came time to announce new regulatory reforms, President Obama showed he had learned a minor lesson—namely, that the OTS was ineffective, so he promised to dismantle it. But the major lesson—that government has no superior power of foresight—eluded him. Echoing President Bush's statement of twenty years earlier, he promised that his new reforms and agencies would "make sure that these problems are dealt with so that we're preventing crises in the future."

It is not just the politicians who succumb to the preconception that government is wiser than the public. Economist George Akerlof is a winner of the Nobel Prize in Economics, and Robert Shiller holds the Arthur M. Okun Chair in Economics at Yale. In *Animal Spirits,* published in 2009, these experts expound their view that the government needs to manage the economy: "Without intervention by the government the economy will suffer massive swings in employment. And financial markets will, from time to time, fall into chaos."

Remarkably—considering that economists are supposed to be scientists—these scholars do not present any evidence whatsoever to support the claim that government can stabilize the economy. Still more remarkable, they have not digested the mountain of evidence that refutes it. The twentieth century is a laboratory of failed government efforts to prevent financial crises. In their book, Akerlof and Shiller note one of the first of these efforts, begun nearly a century ago: the establishment of the Federal Reserve System in 1913. They quote President Wilson, who claimed, in signing the legislation to create the Fed, that it would be a "safeguard against business depressions." Akerlof and Shiller note that this Federal Reserve System was ineffective in preventing the stock-market bubble of the 1920s, ineffective in preventing the crash of 1929, and ineffective in preventing the Great Depression of the 1930s.

The crash and recession of 2008 reinforce the point. These economic crises took place in spite of an alphabet soup of government agencies that were supposed to prevent such problems.

How do Akerlof and Shiller maintain their faith in government management despite a century of failure? They are victims of the watchful eye illusion. We don't have to guess on this point, for they announce their adherence to this perspective in the preface of their book, likening government to a wise parent: "The proper role of the parent is to set the limits so that the child does not overindulge her animal spirits. But those limits should also allow the child independence to learn and to be creative. The role of the parent is to create a *happy home,* which gives the child freedom but also protects him from his animal spirits. This happy home corresponds exactly to . . . our position regarding the proper role of government."

This analogy makes sense only if you assume that the people running the government are parentlike in having greater maturity, judgment, and moral development than everyone else. As soon as you notice they are ordinary politicians—shallow, distracted, and demagogic—then it seems rather silly to imagine that they can intelligently manage an economy.

How Smart Is Big Brother?

One feature of government that encourages us to believe that it must be highly intelligent is its enormous size. We all have heard the truism that two heads are better than one. By this logic, it seems a government agency with thousands of employees and g_gantic databanks must be capable of knowing things that ordinary people cannot possibly master.

We seldom get a chance to put this idea to a quantitative test, though, because government agencies rarely put what they know in testable form. Some years ago, however, the Government Accountability Office (GAO) happened to investigate an agency that was making quantitative predictions, and it issued a report on the accuracy of these predictions. The results are eye opening.

Each year the Department of Agriculture attempts to estimate how much all the farm subsidy programs are going to cost so that it can submit its budget requirements to Congress. To arrive at this prediction, it employs an extensive information-gathering process involving eighteen different units within the department. These different offices funnel information into the decision-making process, including projected supply and demand for commodities, projected prices for commodities, farmer participation in the various subsidy programs, and so on.

The expense of operating this information-gathering system easily runs into the millions of dollars, for it involves numerous subagencies, such as the Foreign Agricultural Service and the Agricultural Marketing Service, as well as budget offices, undersecretaries, and assistant secretaries. Arriving at agricultural projections isn't the only function of these bodies, but it is one of their major responsibilities.

With all these people working on the task, how well does the Department of Agriculture do in forecasting its commodity subsidy costs? The GAO found the estimates for the years 1972–86 were "substantially incorrect," off an average of $4.3 billion, or 59 percent. To put this figure in perspective, if you said that next year's costs would be the same as last year's, your average annual error would be $4.1 billion. In other words, the most simple-minded extrapolation would have done a better job predicting the subsidy expenditures than the department's multimillicn-dollar forecasting system!

Government, it appears, may not be wise and all-knowing at all. If the experience at the Department of Agriculture is an indication, its intellectual competence may be lower than that of an ordinary citizen. The problem is not with the intelligence of the public officials themselves. On an individual basis, they are as bright as the rest of us. It is the system in which they function that creates error.

The problem is that government information systems are not neutral. Every government agency is affected by three biases that lead it to distort findings:

1. The tendency to exaggerate the magnitude of the problem the agency is supposed to address (because the more serious the problem seems, the more necessary will the agency's work seem).
2. The tendency to exaggerate the agency's success (because if people think it is doing a good job, they will reward it with higher appropriations, and an admission of failure is an invitation to be closed down).
3. The tendency to minimize the expected cost of programs (to lure lawmakers and the public into approving these programs).

The last bias played an important role in the Department of Agriculture's mistaken forecasts. Officials feared that if the projected costs of farm subsidies seemed high, opponents might mount a campaign to scale them back. Therefore, they understated the expected cost. Over the fifteen-year period, the average subsidy forecast was $3.1 billion less than the actual cost.

Another problem with government information systems is size. It is not true that more people means more knowledge. Useful knowledge about what will happen in the world doesn't come from collecting more and more facts. It involves rejecting points, too, leaving aside input that is unsound or misleading. Large entities typically lack this ability to discriminate. Their output is often a hodge-podge of different views and watered-down compromises.

Finally, government information systems are often erroneous because no one pays a price for being wrong. In a private business, owners and managers are disciplined for badly mistaken estimates. The restaurant that orders food for one hundred and only serves twenty customers is soon driven out of business. In government agencies, however, tax dollars keep rolling in regardless of performance. As a result, there is no real concern about costly forecasting systems that are routinely wrong.

This blasé attitude is reflected in the GAO's recommendations after it documented the failure of the Agriculture Department's forecasting system. The GAO did not suggest that any Department of Agriculture official be disciplined for the "substantially incorrect" forecasts. It did not recommend reducing appropriations to any unit or cutting anyone's salary as a penalty for the bad performance. Nor did it propose that the department shut down the expensive forecasting system and simply extrapolate costs from the prior year—which, as it noted, would produce somewhat better forecasts. Instead, it gave the insipid advice it routinely gives in its hundreds of reports uncovering government ineptitude: "The [Department of Agriculture] should improve the management of its forecasting processes."

The GAO, you see, is also a government agency, and it goes on being funded year after year no matter how trite and ineffective its recommendations.

Why Regulators Don't Need a License

Before we allow someone to get in the cockpit of a commercial airliner, we apply numerous tests—tests of piloting ability, tests of cognitive skills, and assessments of physical and mental health. The people who fill many other occupations, from truck drivers to plumbers, face similar, if somewhat less demanding, standards. What then, one asks, are the standards set for the people who write government regulations? What examinations do they have to pass?

The surprising answer is that the laws that establish regulatory systems for health, safety, commerce, and transportation do not require that those who write regulations have any definite ability or qualifications. Prospective regulators do not have to pass IQ tests. They do not have to demonstrate that they have analytical minds. They do not have to prove that they have a command of any important body of knowledge. They do not have to demonstrate proficiency in cost-benefit analysis; indeed, they do not even have to have heard of cost-benefit analysis.

In most cases, you become a regulation writer simply by walking off the street and getting a job in a bureaucracy. Regulators often have an informal background in the field, but this experience is not legally required. Fire codes, building codes, plumbing codes, electrical codes, health and safety codes: these regulations are, in almost all cases, drawn up by ordinary people on the basis of their personal judgments and opinions. Yet the accidental damage their regulations can inflict is many times greater than the crash of a plane or truck. Their regulations have the force of the state behind them; they impose fines and jail sentences for noncompliance. Their regulations might cost businesses and consumers millions of dollars, and the indirect effects of unsound regulations can lead to loss of life.

It's a paradox that begs for explanation: Why does society give so much power to untrained, unproven people? The answer, I believe, is the aura of wisdom that envelops all government officials, courtesy of the watchful eye illusion. We worry about pilots or truck drivers making a mistake because they are ordinary people. That's why we want to check on their credentials. We don't worry about regulators making mistakes because we unconsciously assume that government officials are wise and that government actions are always sound and well justified.

If you want to overcome this assumption of government competence, delve into a regulation and try to track down the science and logic that lies behind it. Several years ago I embarked on such an effort in my home community. An "environmental specialist" of the local health district announced new proposed regulations for day care establishments. The aim, Mrs. Jean Hughes told the local newspaper in November, 2000, was to "catch a lot of the smaller daycare centers" and bring them under the jurisdiction of her office. The new rules would require those who care for as few as two children to be licensed. To make sure day care providers were doing the right thing, Mrs. Hughes drafted fifteen pages of regulations, which contained more than 680 requirements, covering everything from posting an "emergency evacuation plan" to keeping hot foods at a temperature higher than 145 degrees.

According to Mrs. Hughes, these regulations were just the beginning, the "foundation" of a still more comprehensive plan of day care regulation incorporating the wish lists of "child care advocates" (meaning the large day care companies that wanted more regulation in order to drive small providers—their competitors—out of business). What made the prospect of this regulatory empire so disturbing was that it appeared to have no basis in science, medicine, or economics. To confirm this suspicion, I went to the health district office and requested a copy of the justification for the regulations. I was told that there was no such document. So I wrote to Mrs. Hughes, challenging her to provide the rationale for her regulations. She failed to reply.

To motivate a response, I published my letter in the local newspaper. It ran as follows:

> *Dear Ms. Hughes:*
>
> *I'm sorry you are not responding to my requests for information about the new day care regulations you are elaborating on behalf of the State of Idaho. Since these regulations will have the force of law and will be backed by police power, it seems to me you have an obligation to be forthcoming about your rationale for imposing them.*
>
> *Thus far, your office has produced only the proposed regulations and not one word of justification. Here are some of the questions you need to answer:*
>
> *1. How many of these "micro" day care establishments that you propose to regulate are there? How many children are in these establishments? (This data is obviously a prerequisite for gauging any effects of regulation.)*

2. *What has been the illness/injury rate of children in the unregulated micro day care establishments compared to the illness/injury rate of children in regulated day care? (In other words, how do you know the regulation is necessary?)*

3. *What scientific evidence exists to show that any of the proposed regulations would actually lower the illness/injury rate in day care establishments? (For example, is there a scientific study that shows that if a day care's hot water has a temperature of, say, 75 degrees—10 degrees less than the proposed regulation—there is more illness in that establishment?)*

4. *What will be the cost to day care operators of implementing the proposed regulations?*

5. *What will be the effect of the increase in costs and red tape on (a) day care costs to parents and (b) closure of day care establishments, and hence the supply of day care?*

6. *To what extent will the regulation and forced closure of micro day care establishments result in a decline in loving environments for children?*

Rational regulation would require clear, documented answers to all of the above questions. Otherwise, you run the risk of implementing regulations that do nothing to enhance the safety, health, or happiness of children in day care, while adding to costs, adding to taxes, and taking away freedom.

I eagerly await your answers.

Sincerely yours,

James L. Payne

There's not much more to tell. The public embarrassment finally motivated Mrs. Hughes to reply to my letter. It was a brief, evasive document that ignored all my questions. In an abrupt reversal, she denied that she had any intention to put forth day care regulations. All she was doing, she said, was "gathering information and input from the public on what the perceived needs and requested areas of enhanced regulations are." In other words, simply demanding that a regulator give sound scientific and economic justifications for her regulations caused her to tear them up and pretend they never existed!

Next time you see a fire code or a sanitary code or a building code, take a closer look. You will see requirements that are not backed by scientific research and have not passed any objective test that demonstrates they do more good than harm. They merely reflect the opinions of the people who wrote them. No one stopped to ask them if they knew what they were doing because, in the grip of the watchful eye fallacy, observers automatically supposed that government has a wise and sound basis for its actions.

Why Children Are Dying in the Nation's Capital

Years ago, ordinary people took care of neglected children. The children were handed over to relatives or neighbors or given to charitable organizations that ran shelters, homes, and adoption programs. These were primitive times, and society was not attuned to the needs of children. Many adopted children were treated harshly, often neglected, and often made to do farm or domestic work. What we need, said reformers, is for government to supervise the handling of orphans to prevent abuses. Over the years, reformers got their way. The first law empowering government to impose its view of what was in the best interest of the child was passed in Massachusetts in 1851. Since that time, states have passed reams of regulations on adoptions, and the federal government has entered the field with twenty-one different laws. Government agencies now manage foster care programs and supervise all adoptions from foster care.

Underlying this movement toward government management was the mindset I have called "the watchful eye illusion." Reformers assumed that government has the skill and foresight to manage orphan problems carefully and responsibly. They believed that it could do a much better job than private groups and individuals which seemed "haphazard."

Now, a century into the process, we have some evidence about how well government agencies care for neglected children. Washington, D.C., the home of big government, has on its own doorstep a glaring case of agency failure. It is Child and Family Services, the unit of the city government that is supposed to take care of abused and abandoned children. Policymakers and editorialists who expect government to save us would profit from taking a close look at the history of this agency.

The minimum expectation for a child welfare agency is that it keep its charges alive. Well, D.C.'s Child and Family Services hasn't been able to accomplish that. As newspaper headlines have been reminding the city for years, the children in its care die—or are killed—in alarming numbers. An investigation by the *Washington Post* found that 229 children ended up dead after coming under the supervision of this agency from 1993 to 2000. In some cases, government workers were informed that a child was in a life-threatening situation, but they failed to follow up. In many others, social workers placed the child in a foster home or institution that was neglectful or abusive. This program, the *Post* concluded in an editorial back in 1991, "has abused the children almost as much as the battered families and broken homes from which they were rescued."

Jolted by screaming headlines, the politicians have thrown money at the problem, but that hasn't worked. With a budget of $147 million, D.C.'s Child and Family Services spends $45,000 a year for each child under supervision. (When a bureaucracy tries to take care of children, it is very expensive!)

Some say that the way to fix agency failure is to write regulations that clearly instruct the employees on what they must do in each case. Well, that's been tried, and it hasn't worked. In fact, overregulation may have made the problem worse. In the early 1990s, it emerged that a social worker dealing with a custody case had to write up and submit nine complex documents within twenty-four hours—a huge deterrent to action.

When all else had failed, the lawyers came with their lawsuits. In 1989, the American Civil Liberties Union (ACLU) filed a class-action suit on behalf of abused and neglected children. That lawsuit dragged along until April 1991, when the U.S. District Court judge hearing the case, Thomas Hogan, concluded that the agency was a "travesty," that it was creating a "lost generation of children whose tragic plight is being repeated every day." This court decision led to a treatylike agreement between the city government and the ACLU lawyers stipulating a number of formal targets (such as preparing a four-hundred-page book of regulations) that Child and Family Services agreed to accomplish.

Years passed. The agency failed to meet most of the formal targets, and lawyers, agency staff, and the judge were bogged down in incessant wrangling. Even the ACLU lawyer who had filed the lawsuit was disenchanted. "There was just an endless process and no results," she said. "We have to go back to court on almost everything." And the system kept on abusing children.

So in May 1995 the judge took control of the agency and put it in the care of a receiver, a court-appointed official given full power over it. At first, there was euphoria. "This is fantastic," said one foster parent familiar with the agency's incompetence and abuses. "There's no way a bureaucracy is going to stop me," said Jerome Miller, the first appointed receiver.

Brave words, but they amounted to very little. By 2001, six years later, Child and Family Services had been through three receivers, yet it still remained, according to the *Washington Post,* "one of the most dysfunctional child protection agencies in the nation." Its adoption and foster care functions are still snarled in delay and misunderstanding, leaving hundreds of children in a perpetual and stressful limbo. Children in the system spend an average of 3.7 years being shunted around in temporary care (the Adoption and Safe Families Act of 1997 mandates that permanent arrangements be made within one year).

The court supervision continues, producing Kafkaesque tangles as the judiciary attempts to micromanage the hapless agency. For example, in October 2001, a federal judge ordered an employee to be jailed for "willful disregard of a court order" requiring her to file reports on two neglected children. The social worker claimed that, being overworked, she didn't have time to write the reports.

She had a point. For more than a decade, the agency has had a problem of inadequate staffing, and every administrator and judge connected with the program has promised to correct it. But they haven't succeeded. The agency has ninety unfilled caseworker positions. It has the money; it just can't retain workers.

In 1999–2000, one-third of its social workers quit, turned off by incompetence, red tape, and micromanagement. After all, who would want to work in an agency where if you don't file your reports, a judge will send you to jail?

In 2008, another shocking error by the agency came to light. On a street in the Washington, D.C., suburb of Calvert, a man spotted a seven-year-old girl dressed in a soiled nightgown, her body covered with bruises. She told him she had escaped from the home where her mother had imprisoned her, starved her, and beaten her. She also reported that this mother had beaten her two sisters to death. The police made a search of the mother's premises and found a freezer where the bodies of two other little girls had been stored for more than a year.

Investigation into this sad affair revealed that these three abused children had been adopted from foster care. It raised a puzzling question: Why did Rene Bowman, the mother, adopt children she had no intention of loving? After all, from a parent's point of view, children can be quite an inconvenience. They cry and disrupt your ability to enjoy quiet time and social activities. They need food, which you have to shop for and prepare, and clothes you have to buy and dress them in. The reason why parents put up with these burdens is that they love the children. If Rene Bowman didn't even like children, if children were just a burden to her, why would she go to the trouble of adopting them?

Reporters did a little more digging and found the answer: she was receiving a subsidy of $2,400 a month, as provided for by the federal Adoption Assistance and Child Welfare Act of 1980. These children—or as was abhorrently so, the dead bodies of these children stored in the freezer—were her way of collecting cash from government (she collected $152,000 in all).

Bowman's was not an isolated case. *Washington Post* columnist Courtland Milloy reported in February 2009 that in the pre-
vious eight months at least seven adopted children in D.C. had
been killed, their adoptive parents charged or suspected in the
homicides. No one knows how many other children being supported by adoption subsidies were being abused and neglected to
a point short of death.

In analyzing what went wrong with adoption subsidies, we
should first note that policymakers were obviously laboring
under the materialistic illusion: they believed that money would
buy socially desirable behavior, and they ignored the importance
of human factors. After all, for the subsidy to work as intended, all
of the adoptive parents would have to be of good character, have
parenting skills, and be motivated to take care of children.

Policymakers' second mistake was succumbing to the watchful eye illusion: they assumed that the government agencies that
were supervising adoptions and distributing the subsidy would be
wise, alert, and thorough. As we have seen, D.C.'s Child and Family Services is none of these things. In the Rene Bowman case, this
agency was supposed to establish that she was a suitable adoptive
parent, and it was supposed to supervise the adoption to see that
everything was going well. In practice, it didn't even notice—or
care—that she had a criminal record, and it knew nothing about
her abuse and murder of the children.

The overall picture, then, is of a government agency that continues to fall grossly short, decade after decade, despite the best-
intentioned efforts to reform it. Judges and administrators keep
promising, and editorialists keep wringing their hands, while
children keep dying. Such is the culmination of a system begun
many generations ago by idealists who earnestly sought to better

the lot of neglected children, but who made the mistake of sup-posing that government is morally, intellectually, and adminis-tratively superior to the arrangements that families, friends, and community groups create on their own.

6

The Illusion of
Government Preeminence

Whatever Happened to Limited Government?

The evolution of American government has been a great disappointment to many conservatives—and a puzzle. They can't understand how a government established on firm lines of restraint should have grown to be so unlimited. The Constitution contains numerous checks and balances to keep government from acting too rapidly, and explicitly limits the role of the federal government. What happened? The answer given in this book is that politicians and the public have succumbed to illusions about what government is and what it can accomplish. Of all the illusions promoting government's growth, the sixth one, which I discuss in this chapter, is perhaps the most important of all.

Humans are a problem-solving species. Having spent millennia grappling with the challenges of existence, we have learned the lesson that there is a tool for every task. If you want to dig a hole, a shovel will solve the problem; to sew a shirt, you use needle and thread; and so on. It is therefore natural that when we contemplate social and economic problems, we assume there must be a way to fix them. It is not like us to see troubles such as unemployment, hunger, and illiteracy and then shrug our shoulders and say that nothing can be done.

When we look about for the machine that's supposed to address society's problems, our gaze falls immediately on government. At first glance, it seems to be the heaven-sent institution for healing social ills. Whatever the problems with education, medical care, science, race relations, and so on, government can address them. Its job, as the Founding Fathers put it in the preamble of the U.S. Constitution, is to "promote the general welfare."

It's not wrong to say that government is a problem-solving machine. Government can address problems, and, after a fashion, it can deal with many of them and sometimes improve things. The fallacy comes in not recognizing that there are *two* mechanisms for promoting the general welfare: government and something else. What happens is that in the excitement of the moment and in our anxiety to "do something" about each vexing national issue, we ignore the other system. This is a serious mistake, of course, because whenever there are two methods of accomplishing a given end, it is irrational to suppose there is only one. If there are two ways to get down a cliff, jumping or taking a stairway, sad indeed is the plight of the person who believes the only alternative is to jump.

When it comes to dealing with national social and economic problems, many people are victims of this kind of one-sided thinking. I call it *the illusion of government preeminence: the belief that government is the only problem-solving institution in society.*

What is society's other problem-solving mechanism? It is the sum of all the individuals and groups working in their diverse ways to make the world around them better. Different names are used to refer to this other system, including *society, civil society,* and the *private sector.* I like the term *voluntary sphere,* which refers to the idea that in this area, force and the threat of force are not employed. Instead, people rely on a host of other approaches, including noble impulses such as generosity, compassion, and idealism, as well as on other more mundane motives, such as the need for sociability, the longing for status, and the desire for material gain.

The voluntary sphere comprises families, friends, and neighbors in their great variety of supportive activities. It includes clubs, churches, civic organizations, volunteer groups, and philanthropists that address community problems. It takes in trades, professions, businesses, and commercial organizations that supply social and economic services. It includes authors, publishers, educators, and scientists who develop productive ideas and bring them before the public. It incorporates public opinion—that is, the evolving tide of knowledge and awareness that shapes culture, institutions, and behavior.

Whenever we discuss government and observe that it is the institution for solving national problems, we tend to overlook the voluntary sphere and its problem-solving capacity. We miss the point that this other system can also do the job of promoting "the general welfare" and might, in many cases, be able to do a better job. If children aren't learning enough in school, for example, we overlook the point that this problem is being addressed by parents, teachers, voluntary groups, writers, researchers, businesses, and philanthropists. A government effort to see that children do better in school might be unnecessary, or it might be ineffective. Or—and this is the biggest danger—it might undermine these voluntary efforts at improvement.

The illusion of government preeminence leads, in the long run, to the demise of limited government. Where the public and the politicians believe that government is the *only* problem-solving institution in society, constitutional restraints will not keep them from turning to it to handle everything. A public in the grip of this illusion believes that it faces a simple choice: use government to address pressing national needs, or do nothing. For a problem-solving species, the choice is a no-brainer.

Statues of Generals, Not of Teachers

The illusion of government preeminence has its source in a number of powerful perceptual biases. The first is the human tendency to focus on big things and to treat large size alone as a virtue. If we take an excursion into the jungle and are later asked to discuss the animals we encountered, of course we shall talk about the elephant. It is most unlikely that we shall mention ants.

Government is the big, prominent institution in the land. It resides in gigantic marble halls that echo with importance. Go to the Capitol building in Washington, D.C., during the spring and see visiting schoolchildren gape in awe at massive metal statues of past politicians. When these children grow up and wonder who will solve the problems of the day, where will their attention fly? In contrast, the voluntary system is not imposing. It is made up of a multitude of small, decentralized units: the local hardware store, the Cub Scouts, your grandmother. It is like the ants of the forest, not really noticeable as a problem-solving system unless you make a special effort to examine it.

Government also has massively visible power. It has millions of police officers and soldiers available to impose its will on the community. Something in the human psyche makes us want to admire those who command the use of force, a bias reflected in the fact that there are many more statues of generals than there are of teachers. The admiration of force may well be declining in modern times, following the general decline in the approval of force noted in chapter 2, but it has not disappeared by any means, and it leads segments of the public to admire the government that commands the ranks of soldiers marching down the avenue. In contrast, the voluntary sphere does not employ physical force. Its units operate on the basis of voluntary exchange, persuasion, exhortation, and generosity. Although these principles are socially valuable, they do not excite instincts of awe the way guns and armies do.

The dynamics of democratic electoral competition reinforce the illusion of government preeminence. Elections focus attention on what *government* can do. Candidates vie with each other in emphasizing the social and economic problems of the day and in promising to use government to fix them. Candidates who say government *should not* be used to solve problems appear negative and unsympathetic, and they tend to be weeded out of the system. As one official put it (in connection with the 2010 health care legislation), "I didn't get elected not to do something."

Electoral campaigns shortchange the mention of the voluntary sphere. It would not make much sense for a candidate to run for office by pointing out that nongovernmental groups, individuals, families, and businesses can solve social problems. That would be like a toothpaste salesman saying that customers don't need his product because they can use the baking soda they already have at home. Successful political candidates promise to use government to address problems and to supply things people want: jobs, affordable health care, affordable housing, job training, higher education, low-cost transportation, green energy, and so forth. It is not their role to point out that systems other than government can and do address these problems. Thus, political campaigns reinforce the idea that only government can provide solutions and fill needs.

Finally, the illusion of government as the exclusive problem solver rests on government's apparent effectiveness: from a distance, it seems to be the institution that can fix things. This impression of effectiveness is, to a large extent, the product of the other illusions discussed in this book. At first glance, it appears that government has vast funds at its disposal (the philanthropic illusion), that it is tolerably efficient in transferring resources (the illusion of the frictionless state), that its many billions should buy the solution to any problem (the materialistic illusion), and that it has the knowledge to devise intricate solutions to national problems (the watchful eye illusion). In this way, the impression of government as the preeminent problem solver is a second-order illusion, one supported by other illusions.

It is understandable, then, that when a national job needs to be done, people should look to the big, powerful, and seemingly effective entity that looms in their field of vision. The forest is covered with leaves, and we want them picked up. How should this be accomplished? The naive mind looks to the elephant; it does not consider that the forest is full of ants that can do the job. If reminded of this possibility, the believer in the elephant will disparage the ants, pointing to their small size. "How can an ant lift a leaf?" he asks. He has not stopped to consider that a group of ants might join together to carry a leaf. He has not considered that each ant might bite off part of a leaf so that in this way millions of ants can move great masses of leaves.

In the same fashion, the idea that the voluntary system can accomplish anything significant seems at first sight implausible. It is only when we consider the vast multitude of entities working toward the same end that we begin to grasp its potential.

Government Fails, but We Can't Stop Using It

Here's a simple example of how the illusion of government preeminence slips into our thinking. An October, 2009, article in the *Washington Post* about health care in China is headlined, "In China, Too, a Health-Care System in Disarray." The article begins with the case of Shen Baohou, a seventy-two-year-old man who had expensive heart surgery. It quotes him as saying that he couldn't afford his two operations and reports that his children helped pay for the cost. "Without them, I don't think I could have had the operation," he says.

Why does this episode illustrate a system "in disarray?" Having family members pay for operations of other family members is a system of financing health care, one of many in the voluntary sphere. It's an arrangement, one can argue, that is morally sensitive, and that also strengthens family ties—a point generally considered to be a social benefit. Family financing is also a system that is vastly more efficient than taxing Mr. Shen's children and cycling the money through a bureaucracy that pays for health care. By the reporter's own account, this voluntary system of family medical assistance worked fine: Mr. Shen had his operation and it was paid for. If the reporter had been able to focus on the voluntary sphere as a problem-solving system, he would have noticed that his example supported the headline, "In China, a Health-Care System that Works Beautifully."

Unfortunately, the reporter had succumbed to the illusion of government preeminence. To his way of thinking, government is the only machine that can address health-care financing needs. Since government wasn't involved in Mr. Shen's case, the system is in "Disarray."

Books that criticize big government but call for more of it are becoming something of a cottage industry these days. One of the more interesting contributions in this genre is Steven Gillon's book *That's Not What We Meant to Do,* published in 2000. Gillon, a historian, is fascinated by the way many highly touted government programs have turned out to be disasters. He enjoys collecting quotations from promoters who promised great things when a measure was passed, but who deplored the outcome decades later, saying, sometimes literally, "That's not what we meant to do." Among the policies he examines are Franklin Roosevelt's Aid to Dependent Children, the war on poverty, the deinstitutionalization of mental patients, the Immigration Act of 1965, and the Campaign Finance Reform Act of 1974. The lesson of these failures, says Gillon, is not to expect too much from government: "No doubt the journey ahead will take us to places we never intended and produce results we never expected. Some of those places and results will be unpleasant and discouraging."

Despite his sober findings, however, Gillon does not conclude that we should turn away from using government to solve problems. Indeed, he takes issue with conservatives who say we should. He is convinced that we must keep trying: "I would not want readers to conclude from these examples that we must abandon our efforts to identify social problems or suspend efforts to use government as a positive force for social change."

It is difficult to account for this curious attachment to government problem solving. The usual—and one would say rational—conclusion to draw from repeated failure is that the agent doing the failing should be avoided in the future. Gillon's entire book is about the failures of government —indeed, he calls them 'catastrophes"—yet his conclusion is that we must keep trying to use that same government to solve problems.

The explanation for this seemingly puzzling stance is the illusion of government preeminence. Gillon is resigned to government because he believes it is the only alternative. "The complexities of modern life," he writes, "will always have the capacity to confound the plans of social planners, but the alternative—to be content to drift along at the mercy of events because we fear that whatever we try will have unintended consequences—is far less attractive."

This is a false choice. The alternative to government action is *not* "to drift along." The alternative is the millions of creators and reformers in the voluntary sphere who are tackling social problems. Gillon is obviously unaware of this sphere or does not grasp its ability to solve public problems. If he had been able to transcend the idea that government is the only problem solver, he might have come to a more balanced conclusion, which he might have expressed thus: "These many cases of government failure should not lead us to give up on solving problems; they strengthen the case for looking to the voluntary sphere instead of to the government for answers."

A similar example of this illusion appears in a 1991 book by David Osborne and Ted Gabler, *Reinventing Government*. Like

Gillon, Osborne and Gabler are disappointed with the way government works, and they report many examples of waste and folly. Yet they refuse to let poor performance influence their opinion of what government can and should do. "We believe deeply in government," they say in their preface. "Think of the problems facing American society today: drug use; crime; poverty; homelessness; illiteracy; toxic waste; the specter of global warming; the exploding cost of medical care. How will we solve these problems? By acting collectively. How do we act collectively? Through government."

Here in black and white is the illusion of government preeminence. The voluntary sphere is addressing all of the problems the authors note—including global warming: those who believe that carbon dioxide causes global warming and who want to retard this warming are finding ways to reduce the emission of carbon dioxide, working as individuals, in groups, and through commercial firms. Individuals and groups are also working to address drug abuse, illiteracy, the cost of medical care, and so on.

Osborne and Gabler miss this point because they apparently cannot conceive of any way to solve collective problems except through government. Had they overcome the underlying illusion, they would have said, "How do we act collectively? Sometimes through government and sometimes through the creative energy of individuals, families, groups, neighborhoods, and companies."

This level of understanding, in turn, would have led them to reconsider how "deeply" they needed to believe in government.

The Reformers Who Needed a Tennis Star

One reason why we overlook problem solving within the voluntary sphere is that it takes so many diverse and subtle forms. It ranges from a new idea developed by a worker in a specialized trade to the mass production of a needed product by a large company, from the habits that millions of parents instill in their children to an innovative approach to social assistance adopted by a local church. Whereas government is a single, centralized problem solver, the voluntary sphere is a complex, decentralized system that extends beyond imagination.

To illustrate the complexity of this voluntary sphere, it is useful to take a close look at a specific example, a case that comes from the struggle against racial discrimination. Today, when we think of the achievements in this field, our attention goes to government. Indeed, we usually refer to this effort as the "civil rights" movement, a phrase that points to legal measures. From a distance, it can seem that what happened was that the government passed laws to guarantee "civil rights" to blacks, which ended racial discrimination.

In reality, the campaign against discrimination was waged mainly in the voluntary sphere by reformers who undertook a complex, extensive effort of persuasion that goes back many generations. Government's laws were merely the icing on the cake. After all, laws don't drop from the sky. They are an expression of public sentiment. In a democracy, laws against discrimination can be approved only because a majority already believes that discrimination is wrong. A century ago majorities believed that discrimination was fitting. These majorities expressed their sentiments in laws that imposed discrimination against blacks— laws that said that blacks had to ride in the back of the bus, drink only from a certain water fountain, and so on. If opinion hadn't changed, the laws could not have changed.

So the explanation for the new laws goes back to the people who undertook a campaign of persuasion based on voluntary methods. Farsighted individuals of both races worked to change attitudes, laboring in many different spheres, including religion, education, business, entertainment, journalism, and literature. Let's take a close look at one corner of this campaign: the effort to integrate women's tennis.

In 1950, the "color bar" was broken in women's tennis by black athlete Althea Gibson, who played in a tournament put on by the previously all-white United States Lawn Tennis Association. This seemingly simple event had a long, careful development, much of which Gibson—who told her story in her book *I Always Wanted to Be Somebody*—didn't learn about until many years later.

Gibson was a New York City runaway and high school dropout who spent her time in street games. When she was growing up in the early 1940s, the Harlem section of New York had a strong black elite that supported numerous voluntary associations. One of them was the Cosmopolitan Tennis Club, "the ritzy [black] tennis club in Harlem," as Gibson describes it. She was invited to play there, with her junior membership and tennis lessons paid for by club donors and volunteers. She explains how Mrs. Rhoda Smith took her under her wing. "Rhoda is a well-off society woman who had lost her own daughter about ten years before I met her, and she practically adopted me. She bought me my first tennis costume and did everything she could to give me a boost." This assistance included improving Althea's table manners and social graces so she could behave presentably in the more refined world of tennis. Another voluntary association important in Gibson's career was the predominantly black American Tennis Association, which organized the tournaments in which she played.

In 1946, when Gibson turned eighteen, two black doctors, Hubert A. Eaton and Robert W. Johnson, made an unusual arrangement. Gibson describes it: "The plan they finally came up with was for me to leave New York City and go to Wilmington, North Carolina, to live with Dr. Eaton during the school year, go to high school there, and practice with him on his private back-yard tennis court. In the summer I would live with Dr. Johnson in Lynchburg and I would travel with him in his car to play the [black] tournament circuit. Each doctor would take me into his family as his own child and take care of whatever expenses came up during the part of the year I was with him."

Why were they doing this? Doctors Eaton and Johnson were more than kindly tennis buffs who wanted to encourage an up-and-coming player. They were social reformers who had a long-range plan for bringing down the color bar in tennis, and Gibson was the key. "They already were hoping," Gibson explains, "that I might just possibly turn out to be the Negro player they had been looking for to break into the major league of tennis and play in the white tournaments."

After three years of education and training, Gibson was ready, and the time was right. The top leaders of the black American Tennis Association made a push for the all-white United States Lawn Tennis Association to accept a qualified black player. They felt there was enough popular support for the general idea, and in Gibson they had an athlete who could make a good impression both on and off the court. Dozens of black leaders took up the campaign, writing to the officers of the white tennis organizations and visiting with them to urge the opening up of tennis.

The reaction was mixed. Some in the white tennis community were opposed to integration, afraid that the admission of blacks would change the character of the game. But others became strong supporters of Gibson's cause. Alice Marble, the woman's tennis champion of the day, wrote a firm editorial in *American Lawn Tennis* magazine urging Gibson's case. "If tennis is a game for ladies and gentlemen," she said, "it's also time we acted a little more like gentlepeople and less like sanctimonious hypocrites."

The campaign of persuasion bore fruit. In the summer of 1950, the local white clubs invited Gibson to regional tournaments so that she could be ranked in the white league. In this way, she succeeded in earning an invitation to the nationals at Forest Hills that fall (she was defeated in the second round that year, but won the tournament in 1957). The racial integration of women's tennis had been achieved—not through the compulsion of legislation, but through persuasion and good will.

This kind of achievement goes relatively unnoticed. Instead, history textbooks, influenced by the illusion of government preeminence, mark the success of the movement against discrimination in political terms. They point to a particular law, such as the Civil Rights Act of 1964, as the solution to the problem and show a picture of politicians standing around for a photo-op at the bill-signing ceremony. They do not have a picture of Rhoda Smith or of Hubert Eaton or of the hundreds of officers and volunteers in the different tennis associations who quietly worked to reshape national attitudes and practices. Students reading the textbook naturally come away with the impression that they must look to government to solve national problems.

Crushing the Good Samaritan

Those who see government as the exclusive problem solver overlook the valuable work that the voluntary sphere can do. They also overlook the closely related point that *government action generally displaces and weakens action in the voluntary sphere.* The two problem-solving methods do not compete on a plane of equality. Government deploys force; the voluntary sphere does not. Government is the elephant, easily able to muscle aside or crush any ants in its path. In the long run, government can virtually destroy the voluntary sphere, turning our illusion into a description of reality. Where government has taken control of—or destroyed—all the independent businesses, churches, professions, volunteer groups, writers, newspapers, scientists, and so on, it really will be the case that government is the exclusive problem solver in the country. This condition of total government control is approached in traditional Communist regimes such as North Korea.

The Western democracies are far from this extreme outcome, but even so, one can notice how the growing government role has displaced voluntary action. Government weakens the voluntary sphere in three ways: (1) by seizing roles; (2) by commanding resources; and (3) by depriving the voluntary sphere of freedom of action through its regulations.

To illustrate the first point, look at what has happened on the welfare front. A century ago the care of the poor was in the hands of a vast network of voluntary groups and systems of "volunteer visitors." Each city had a central clearinghouse, known as the "charity organization society" that screened applicants for aid and that coordinated the efforts of the many local charities and churches. In addition, there were large and vital workers' mutual aid societies that supplied medical help, disability support, and retirement income. This is not the place to discuss whether these private arrangements were more effective, efficient, or compassionate than governmental ones. I only observe that as government took for itself the role of caring for the needy, especially with the New Deal, these private arrangements began to whither, so that today they are but a shadow of their former selves.

The second point, that government takes resources from the voluntary sphere is an algebraic truism. Every dollar government takes away from the public in taxes is one less dollar that the private sector has to spend. Let's illustrate how this equation might play out in the case of efforts to help low-income people feed themselves.

One such effort might be a church soup kitchen. Its funds come from donations made by supporters. When government increases taxes on those supporters—to pay for its food program—these donors have less income left to give to the food kitchen, so the voluntary system's antihunger effort is undermined by government's action.

Another feeding effort might be a low-priced restaurant that sells a fish dinner for a dollar less than any other restaurant in town. In this way, the woman operating the restaurant has taken a step to combat hunger, helping to make her customer's food dollar go farther. With her lower prices, a family of six that used to share three dinners might now be able to afford four dinners. If government has the idea that it wants to feed low-income people, too, it can do so only by taxing away money from citizens, including this restaurant owner, thus adding to her costs. This may force her to raise prices or even to close her business. In this way, government's antihunger program impairs the voluntary one.

Government's third burden on the voluntary sphere lies in its regulations, which can have stultifying effects even more injurious than its taxes.

One morning some time ago a shocking e-mail message popped up on my computer screen. It was from Teresa, the president of a volunteer group we had just started to provide after-school activities for teenagers. The subject line was, "Liability Issues and Board Function," her way of alluding to the many legal threats and challenges that loomed over our small-town charity. It said: "Hello Friends of Sandpoint Teen Center. I am resigning from the board of Sandpoint Teen Center effective immediately."

The message was shocking because Teresa was the heart and soul of the teen center. She had felt drawn to these youngsters with their stringy hair and too-long jeans, seeing them at loose ends after school, so ready to drift into drugs, alcohol abuse, and crime, and felt impelled to do something. Her tireless recruiting drew in board members and other volunteers, and her eager telephoning brought us our first donations. She worked at the center almost every day, greeting the youngsters, playing ping-pong with them, and leading the moment of silence before snack time.

Though Teresa's message was shocking, it was not surprising. A volunteer who tries to set up a human services organization in this country quickly discovers she is entering a jungle of government regulation. This jungle is expensive to negotiate, requiring the assistance of lawyers, tax accountants, and insurance agents, as well as vast amounts of paperwork. Large nonprofits have bureaucracies in order to stay on top of and defend against government officials' demands, but newcomers have no such protection. They stand alone and unprotected, fearful that a legal misstep might, in an extreme case, deprive them of their property or land them in jail. This was how Teresa saw it in explaining her decision to resign. "I can't jeopardize our home," she told me.

Our group got a first taste of regulation when we tried to open a bank account. Because of new regulations from the U.S. Department of Homeland Security, we were required to get an employer identification number. Who was going to sign the application for the number and be responsible to the IRS? I finally agreed to be the guinea pig. As it turned out, the IRS added insult to injury: just to get the number cost our group $88.

Board members started asking, "Do we have 501(c)(3) status?" This expensive and burdensome paperwork, which began as an IRS device to regulate the charitable tax deduction, has taken on a life of its own in the voluntary sector. Many volunteers assume you aren't a legal voluntary group unless you have it. Others believe it is illegal to raise funds without it, an impression reinforced by donors who keep asking if the group has 501(c)(3) status.

We worried about lawsuits. Parents might sue us if a kid crushed his finger playing air hockey or if he fell off his bike after he left the center or if we authorized emergency medical treatment without formal permission. We knew we needed costly liability insurance, but how many different kinds of insurance did we need? On one occasion, a volunteer suggested taking some teens down the street to rake leaves for a shut-in grandmother. "No," someone else said, "we can't do that because we don't have liability insurance for off-premises activities."

We became aware of pressures from state and federal agencies. They might prosecute us for failing to adhere to requirements on nondiscrimination, or the Americans with Disabilities Act. A circular mailed to us pointed out that under the new Sarbanes-Oxley Act, charity board members can face criminal prosecution for alleged lapses in financial management and financial disclosure.

The anxiety came to a head at a board meeting. Participants reviewed the aforementioned challenges and brought to light some new ones. One woman feared we were subject to Occupational Safety and Health Administration regulations and might be fined if our rented space was found in violation. Another volunteer thought we needed a state permit for a commercial kitchen because we prepared nachos for the kids in our little oven. The hiring of a part-time employee brought upon us requirements of withholding and depositing tax payments: Who would undertake to manage this problem? In this connection, one board member told a frightening tale. She was a bookkeeper for a small firm that went bankrupt, and the IRS came to her for missing taxes. "I had to hire a lawyer to defend myself," she said, "and take out a second mortgage on my house to pay for it. I'm never going to go through that again." It was a very depressing meeting, and it was not surprising that it would lead a board member to resign.

Government's heavy regulatory hand inflicts this kind of unintended injury all over the country millions of times a year. For another example, consider the case of Mary Lisch, who ran a day care business in Fairfield, California. Lisch was a remarkable woman. Born without arms, she learned to use other parts of her body, especially her feet, head, and chin to accomplish the ordinary tasks that most people take for granted. Reporter Pamela Martineau of the *Sacramento Daily Bee* visited with Mrs. Lisch in 1996 and was impressed with her clever techniques for taking care of children.

Working from a tall stool in the center of her kitchen, Lisch sliced fruit and prepared other snacks for kids using the feet that for all her life have stood for her missing hands. "I probably wash my feet 50 to 100 times a day," she said, laughing. Besides providing care for children who might otherwise have gone home to an empty house after school, Lisch was a role model for overcoming a disability.

"She certainly gave the children a great awareness that a handicap doesn't mean anything," one parent was quoted as saying in the September 20, 1996 article. "She proved that anyone can do anything," said a teenager who went to Lisch's establishment as a toddler. A father of a four-year-old attending the school said, "It was obvious she loved the children."

For Lisch, caring for children was a mission: "I just don't believe in warehousing children," she said. "They need to be in a home environment."

Lisch ran her after-school care center for twenty years, for the first nine below government's radar. Then state regulators noticed her and forced her to be licensed and inspected. Year by year she struggled to keep up with each new requirement, but state officials finally pulled out an ace: she had to be certified in cardiopulmonary resuscitation (CPR)—an insuperable obstacle to a person with no arms. Mary was forced to close her day care center, a move that was as hard on her as on the children deprived of her services. "I felt absolutely worthless," she said. "It took me three or four weeks to get used to not having anything to get up for."

So government drove this saint of California day care out of business, a result no one intended, not even Jeanine Hillman, the licensing supervisor of the California Department of Social Services. Hillman felt the CPR requirement was unjustified and would eventually have been waived if Lisch had had the time, money, and energy to fight it all the way through the bureaucracy. The elephant regretted crushing the ant.

Impelled by the illusion that government is society's only problem solver, the politicians year by year endorse ever more regulations to prevent bad things from happening. People might fall on faulty stairs, so they set up an agency to punish people who own buildings with broken steps or encourage liability lawyers to sue the pants off people responsible for broken steps. For those who see the world only from government's viewpoint, the system is well-intended. They fail to recognize, however, the quiet, long-run mischief that government action inflicts on the voluntary sphere. All regulations have a depressing side effect: in order to act against supposed bad apples, government officials have to burden and intimidate millions of well-intentioned and perfectly innocent people engaged in creative, compassionate action. With their gaze fixed on malefactors, lawmakers overlook the impact of their penalties on the world's benefactors. They drive Teresa from the teen center; they close down Mary's program of after-school care.

Conclusion: A Philanthropist Goes to Washington

In philanthropy, as in other human undertakings, there are degrees of performance, from inspired to disappointing. Because the very act of generosity merits some credit, we are reluctant to give an entirely negative rating to any donor, but sometimes a philanthropist comes along who tests our forbearance. The case I'm thinking of is Ruth Lilly, heiress to the Eli Lilly pharmaceutical fortune, who in 2002 announced a gift of $120 million to support the arts.

If you had $120 million and wanted to assist the arts, how would you do it? Well, you could identify twelve thousand artists and give $10,000 to each one. Or you could give the money to art museums, theater companies, art schools, and so on. Ruth Lilly and her lawyers had a different idea. She donated the entire $120 million to an organization called Americans for the Arts. This organization is a pressure group that lobbies for taxpayer funding of the arts: most of its "members" are the state and local government arts agencies that get the taxpayer funding. Its main effort is a yearly campaign to urge Congress to pass higher appropriations for the federal arts agency, the National Endowment for the Arts (NEA). From its offices on Vermont Avenue and K Street, Americans for the Arts organizes teams of lobbyists and celebrities who, the *Washington Post* reports, "fan out across Capitol Hill, calling on members of Congress and other key officials."

In other words, instead of supporting the arts directly and giving her money to artists, Ruth Lilly gave her funds to (*a*) an organization that is (*b*) supposed to lobby Congress, which is (*c*) supposed to give tax dollars to a government agency that is (*d*) supposed to give it to artists. What led her to this convoluted approach? My explanation is that she and her lawyers and advisors were in the grip of many illusions about government.

Let's start with the *philanthropic illusion*. As noted in chapter 1, contrary to the popular belief, government does not have any wealth of its own. Its subsidy programs simply transfer it. They take money away from Americans who were going to spend it on worthy causes of their own choosing—food, housing, travel, business investment, education—and transfer it to the beneficiaries of the subsidy program. Hence, what Ruth Lilly was trying to buy is an enhancement of the system of robbing Peter to pay Paul the arts administrator. Because the biggest taxpayers are wealthy individuals, the Peters being robbed are, to a large extent, her fellow philanthropists who, if allowed to keep their money, would, among other things, donate generously to the arts. Hence, to the degree that the lobbying succeeded, Ruth Lilly was preventing her fellow Americans from spending their money on their own needs, hopes, and dreams, *including the arts*.

The voluntary illusion. We must further observe that the transaction Ruth Lilly sought to foster was a coercive one. Probably without fully realizing it, she was seeking to make use of government to threaten Americans with imprisonment in order to force them to give money to the NEA. A person in the grip of the voluntary illusion would not notice this unsavory aspect. She would make the hazy assumption that wealth flows into the Treasury through some automatic, benign process.

The illusion of the frictionless state. The next problem with Lilly's lobbying approach to supporting the arts was waste. Government subsidy systems have huge overhead costs. These costs include the burdens placed on the economy in the form of tax compliance, enforcement, and litigation costs as well as disincentives to production. As noted in chapter 3, these overhead costs of taxation can be conservatively estimated at sixty-five cents for every tax dollar collected. In addition, there is the overhead and waste in the disbursement process, including everything from grant application and administration costs on the private sector to overhead in the government agencies. For example, the NEA spends only about half its appropriations in actual grants to artists and art projects. The rest is eaten up in administrative overhead and money the agency spends in lobbying and self-advertisment. Overall, there is something like a three-to-one waste factor in the NEA tax-and-spend system, compared to a system where consumers and philanthropists are allowed to support art directly with their own money.

The materialistic illusion. As the great philanthropists have observed, it is harder to give money away creatively and effectively than it is to earn it. These philanthropists invest enormous time and thought into developing methods to assist worthy causes.

Alas, philanthropists not willing to make this personal investment fall victim to the materialistic illusion, the belief that dumping money in someone else's lap purchases a successful outcome.

The watchful eye illusion. Ruth Lilly and her advisors probably felt that they didn't have the expertise to know which artists should be rewarded and which ignored. They therefore needed some way to turn this task over to experts. Where are the experts to be found? If you are swayed by the watchful eye illusion, you will suppose government officials are specially qualified to decide what is and isn't "Great Art." If you transcend that illusion, however, you notice that government officials can be as biased and self-centered as anyone else. In awarding subsidies, they are likely to establish procedures that reward insiders, personal friends, and the politically well connected.

Ruth Lilly's tactic of funding lobbying in order to boost tax funding for the NEA was thus a highly questionable venture, intellectually, morally, and economically. Moreover, it appears to have been a failure politically. Politics is a complex, highly uncertain realm. Hiring lobbyists to push for an increase in funding for an agency doesn't mean that the increase will materialize. In the case of the NEA, it didn't. In five years after the Lilly gift, 2002 to 2007, NEA funding increased by only 8 percent. In the preceding five years, before the Lilly gift, NEA funding increased by 16 percent. Apparently, then, Ruth Lilly wasted her $120 million. Instead of supporting twelve thousand artists, her donation achieved nothing, and all that remains of it are wistful memories of celebrity visits to congressional offices.

Adding to the bitter taste of the episode, a year after Ruth Lilly made the donation, Americans for the Arts sued her estate for more money, claiming that trustees had not managed her assets properly. The suit was essentially frivolous, and was rejected by the Indiana probate court which heard the case. Nothing daunted, Americans for the Arts took the case to an appeals court, which also rejected it, and then to the Indiana Supreme Court, which also turned it down. So part of Ruth Lilly's gift to Americans for the Arts was used to fund lawyers to sue her estate!

When considering what propelled Ruth Lilly to adopt the profoundly unpromising idea of financing a political pressure group to increase government funding for the arts, one can't help but think that, in addition to being in the grip of the illusions already mentioned, she was also influenced by the *illusion of government preeminence.* Her thinking was shaped by the unconscious idea that government is the country's natural problem-solving system. In essence, she said, "Let the elephant do the job because, after all, who else is there?"

We need constantly to remind ourselves that society has two systems for grappling with problems, government and the voluntary sphere, the great multitude of independent entities extending beyond anyone's imagination in numbers and complexity. Reaching for government to solve problems almost inevitably inflicts harm on the voluntary system, by robbing it of function, by extracting resources from it, and by imposing coercive regulations that burden and demoralize it.

Government or the voluntary system: you can't endorse both problem-solving systems at the same time. Society will consider one system to be the "real" one and the other as something incidental. It will have one dominant answer to the question, How do we act collectively?

Today, the prevailing answer to this question is, "Government." Youngsters are taught that government is the agency that makes a better world, and they are urged to go into politics and use the power of the state to right wrongs. This focus on government has blocked a proper appreciation of the voluntary sphere—so much so that most people, including scholars such as Gillon, Osborne, and Gabler, cannot conceive of any way to address social problems except through government. They believe that giving up on the government approach means giving up on working for a better world.

Thus, at the beginning of the twenty-first century we find a curious paradox of values. The politicians, the public, and the intellectuals roundly ignore the voluntary sphere—the social problem-solving system that incorporates the values they advocate. It is voluntary, human scale, efficient, personal, and flexible. Instead, they place their hopes in government, the system whose features they deplore. It is large, coercive, centralized, inefficient, and impersonal. It is also a system that, as even its advocates concede, is highly error prone.

How have multitudes of sincere, idealistic people come to view this distasteful, convoluted system as superior to the voluntary approach? The answer, I submit, is that their thinking has been distorted by six political illusions.